Mallory
on the
Move

Absolutely, Positively 100% for Becca and Adam
—L. F.

For Olivia
—T. S.

Text copyright © 2004 by Laurie B. Friedman
Illustrations copyright © 2004 by Tamara Schmitz

Darby Creek
A division of Lerner Publishing Group, Inc.
241 First Avenue North
Minneapolis, MN 55401 USA

For reading levels and more information, look up this title at www.lernerbooks.com.

Library of Congress Cataloging-in-Publication Data

Friedman, Laurie B.
   mallory on the move / by Laurie B. Friedman ; illustrations by Tamara Schmitz.
      p.   cm.
   Summary: After moving to a new town, eight-year-old mallory keeps throwing stones in the "wishing Pond" but things will not go back to the way they were before, and she remains torn between old and new best friends.
   ISBN 978-1-57505-538-1 (lib. bdg. : alk. paper)
   ISBN 978-1-57505-789-7 (eb pdf)
   [1. moving, Household—Fiction. 2. Best friends—Fiction. 3 . Friendship—Fiction. 4. wishes—Fiction. 5. Family life—Fiction.] I. Schmitz, Tamara, ill. II. Title.
PZ7.F89773mal 2004
[Fic]—dc21   2003008937

Mallory
ON THE
Move

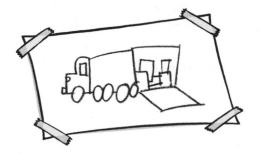

by Laurie Friedman
illustrations by Tamara Schmitz

MINNEAPOLIS

CONTENTS

A WORD FROM MALLORY

moving is a big deal!

When you move, everything changes: your house, your neighborhood, your town, and, worst of all, your friends.

And no one asks if you want to move. It would be nice if your parents said: "Hey, we're thinking about moving. That means you'll have to get used to a new house in a new neighborhood in a new town. You'll have to make all new friends. But we won't do it unless it's OK with you. What do you say?"

Nope. That's not how it happens at all.

First, your parents start whispering to each other.

Then, they have lots of conversations behind closed doors.

Finally, the big day comes. Your parents tell you to sit down. They have an announcement to make. You're moving! And as fast as you can snap your fingers, it's all been decided for you.

I know. I'm Mallory McDonald (like the restaurant but no relation). Age 8 ½ plus 1 month. And that's exactly what happened to me.

When my parents told me I had to move, I asked if they were joking. Everybody knows I love a good joke. But I knew with one look, it was no joke.

And then I got mad. REALLY MAD!

"You ruined my life!" I screamed at my parents. "I'm not moving, and if you try to make me, I'm running away from home!"

Mom told me that running away from home was the same thing as moving, except you have to cook all your own meals. I don't know how to cook.

That's when I knew I was stuck moving.

PACKING

My room is filled with boxes.

Yesterday it was filled with stuffed animals and books and posters. Today it is filled with boxes that are filled with stuffed animals and books and posters.

I'm supposed to be filling more boxes with my stuff. But I don't get it. If I don't want to move, how come I'm stuck packing?

What I need is a helper. I yell from the top of the stairs.

"Mom!"

I wait for an answer. But I don't get one so I use my outdoor voice.

"MOM!"

She comes to the bottom of the stairs with an armload of boxes.

"Hey, Mom, what's big and brown and empty?"

"Mallory, I don't have time for jokes," Mom says. "We have to pack. We're moving in two days."

"I know. But what's big and brown and empty?"

Mom blows a piece of hair out of her mouth. "What?"

"The boxes in my room!" I laugh out loud.

"Mallory, that's about as funny as an overflowing toilet."

I happen to think an overflowing toilet is

hilarious. But I can see Mom doesn't.

"Please go pack," she says.

"But I don't want to move to Fern Falls."
I whimper like a sad, cold puppy left
outside in the rain.

Mom looks at me like she can't decide
what to do. Then she puts her boxes down
and walks up the stairs. "Cheer up." She
pats me on the head. "I'll help."

I sit on the bed with my cat, Cheeseburger.
We watch Mom take T-shirts and shorts
from my drawers. She folds them neatly
and puts them in a big box. When the box
is full, she tapes it shut and writes *Mallory's
T-shirts and shorts* on the outside with a fat
purple marker.

I think over the plan Mary Ann and I
came up with: *Operation-Convince-My-Mom-
that-Moving-and-Leaving-Behind-My-Best-
Friend-Is-a-Bad-Idea.*

Mom starts folding a pile of blue jeans.

I pull a clipboard and a pencil out of the drawer in my night table. "Mom, I have something I need to discuss with you."

She stops folding.

I cross my toes. I hope this works.

"Mary Ann and I have been planning this summer for a long time. We have a very busy schedule." I read from my clipboard.

"Mondays: paint toenails and cat claws.

"Tuesdays: bake cookies and cat treats."

I smile at Mom. I don't tell her we'll need her help with the oven on Tuesdays.

"Wednesdays: work on our summer scrapbook.

"Thursdays: go swimming!"

I remember what Mary Ann told me. *Just read the list.* I don't mention to Mom that before we go swimming, we need to go bathing suit shopping.

Mary Ann said the best time to mention the bathing suit thing is on the way to the swimming pool.

"Fridays: sleepover at Mary Ann's house.

"Saturdays: sleepover at my house.

"Sundays: watch movies in our pajamas all day."

I look up from my clipboard. Mom looks like she swallowed an olive.

I can't tell if that's a good sign or a bad sign. "As you can see from this very busy schedule, I don't have time to move this summer." I shrug my shoulders. "Sorry. Maybe we can talk again in the fall."

"Mallory..." Mom starts to say something. But I don't let her get too far. I can see the plan isn't working like Mary Ann and I thought it would. I switch to Plan B.

"Mom, have you thought this through?" I try to stay calm, but my voice sounds like

it's starting to get upset. "What about your students?"

"There are plenty of good piano teachers in town." Mom folds a pair of jeans across her lap.

"Please!" I get down on my hands and knees. "Please, please, please, please, can we please not move?"

Mom puts the jeans in a box. "Mallory, how many times do we have to go over this?"

My brother, Max, comes in my room and sits down on my dresser. "Somewhere between a hundred and a thousand is my guess," he says. "She's kind of thick for a kid her age. If you know what I mean."

Max thinks he's so smart just because he's ten. I get up off the floor and try pulling him by his feet to get him off my dresser. "Mom!" I moan. "Do something!"

But she can't. Her head is inside a box.

Max tosses a baseball in the air and catches it without looking. "It's simple," he says. "We're moving because Dad is opening a new store in Fern Falls."

"Simple for you," I say. "You don't care where you live. All you care about is baseball. You'll find a new team. It's a lot harder to find a new best friend."

"You're lucky," says Max. "You won't have to be best friends with Birdbrain anymore."

I know Max is talking about Mary Ann. We've lived next door to each other since we were born, and we do everything together. We go to the same school. We chew the same kind of gum. We even paint our toenails the same color.

I cross my arms across my chest. "Mary Ann has been my best friend forever, and I want to keep it that way."

"You might miss Mary Ann," says Max. "But I sure won't."

Mom takes her head out of the box. "Max, please go get more tape."

"I'm not moving to Fern Falls," I tell her when Max is gone.

I sit down on the box Mom is packing. "You and Dad and Max can go. I'll stay here and live with Mary Ann. She said her mom will be glad to have the company since it's just the two of them now."

Mom sits down on the box next to me. "I know you don't want to leave Mary Ann.

And I know she's had a hard time since her parents' divorce. But you'll make new friends. And so will she."

Mom picks up my hand and squeezes it. "Don't forget, Mary Ann can come visit. Fern Falls is only three hours away."

Max comes back in my room and tosses the tape to Mom. "No visits! Please! I've been waiting my entire life to get away from Birdbrain. My wish is finally coming true. Don't ruin it now."

"Max, that's enough." Mom puts her arm around me and pulls me toward her. "Why don't you tell me your joke about the laughing cow?"

"Maybe some other time," I tell her.

It's a funny joke. But moving is no laughing matter.

BLUE WITHOUT YOU

"Rise and shine, Sweet Potato."

I feel someone sit down on my bed. I don't have to open my eyes to know it's Mom. She's the only one who calls me Sweet Potato.

"Knock, knock," I mumble.

"Who's there?" she says.

"Leaf."

"Leaf who?"

"Leaf me alone. . . . I WANT TO SLEEP!" I groan. "Five more minutes."

"We have to finish packing," says Mom.

I roll over and pull the covers over my face. But Mom sticks her head under so she can see me. "Did you forget what's happening today?"

My party! Mary Ann is giving a good-bye party for me. Lots of kids are coming. She told them all to bring presents. I hop out of bed. Now I'm ready to pack!

Mom hands me a list, and we start filling boxes. Sweaters. Socks. Underwear. I check things off the list as we go. Snow boots. Scrapbooks. Bead collection.

My room looks more like a warehouse than a bedroom.

When the phone rings, I run down the hall. "I'll get it!" I yell over my shoulder.

Anything is better than packing.

"Hello," I say.

"Hey, hey, hey," says a familiar voice. "Can you come over now? It's almost time for the party."

"I'll be right over."

I race back to my room. "Mom, can I go to Mary Ann's now? Please? Please? Please?"

Mom smiles and tells me to have fun, fun, fun.

I walk next door with Cheeseburger and knock on Mary Ann's window. She opens it

just a crack. "Password, please."

I whisper through the crack.

Mary Ann flings opens her window, and Cheeseburger and I climb inside. She gives me a big hug and Cheeseburger a little hug. "I'm so, so, so sad today is your last day."

Mary Ann and I always say things three times. It was Mary Ann's idea. She says it shows we've got style.

Mary Ann puts her box of polishes on the floor. "Want to paint our toenails for the party?"

"Purple?" I say. Purple is our favorite color.

"Not today." Mary Ann picks out a bottle of baby blue polish. "Today is blue day."

While we're painting, Max sticks his head in the window. "Hey, Birdbrain, don't even think about planning any visits."

"If I make any visits, it won't be to see

you!" Mary Ann gets up and shuts her window.

"Ready for the party?" she says.

She must be kidding. She knows I can't wait!

Mary Ann puts her hands over my eyes. "OK. No peeking." She walks me down the hall.

I can't see a thing. When she moves her hands, I rub my eyes. Everything in her living room is blue!

There are blue streamers and blue balloons hanging from the ceiling. There is a blue table cloth on the table and blue plates and cups and napkins.

Even the food is blue. Little bowls of blue Jell-O and blue M&Ms and blue jelly beans on the pizza.

There's a big sign hanging over the fireplace. *We'll be BLUE without you!*

"Wow!" I say. "It's hard to feel *BLUE* when I'm with you!" But I do feel blue. I know tomorrow I won't be with Mary Ann anymore.

Mary Ann's mom tells Mary Ann and me to get together. We put our arms around each other, and she snaps our picture. "We'll send you one for the scrapbook," she says.

The doorbell rings, and Mary Ann opens the door. The guests begin to arrive. They all have on blue T-shirts.

We eat pizza. Then Mary Ann says, "Does anyone have anything for Mallory?"

Becca Birdwell gives me an address book. "So you won't forget us when you move." She writes her address in the book and passes it around the room.

Claudia Thompson gives me a cat-of-the-month calendar. Everybody knows I love cats.

Emily and Ellen Edwards give me a candle that looks like a cheeseburger. There are layers of lettuce and pickles and tomatoes. There's even a meat and a bun layer. It looks so real I could eat it.

"Open mine," says Stephanie Sanders. She gives me a joke book.

I flip through the pages and stop at the section with cat jokes. I pick up Cheeseburger and cover her ears. "What do you call a mad cat?"

No one knows.

"A crabby tabby!

Everybody laughs.

I read another one. "What do you call a fat cat?"

I pause. "A flabby tabby."

"Funny! Funny! Funny!" says Mary Ann. Then she hands me another box. It's wrapped in purple paper with a purple bow. "From me," she says.

I tear the paper off slowly. I lift the lid off a small box. Inside are two bottles of light purple glitter polish. I read the card.

Roses are red and violets are blue.

One is for me and one is for you.

Mary Ann takes one of the bottles of polish out of the box and stuffs it in her pocket. "No matter where we live, our toes will always match."

I hug Mary Ann and promise never to wear anything else.

When Mom comes to get me, Mary Ann's mom asks about the family that bought our house.

"They have a son who's eight," Mom tells her.

"Perfect," says Mary Ann's mom. "There will be somebody on the street for Mary Ann to play with."

Mary Ann leans over and grabs her stomach. "Me! Play with a boy! I'm going to be sick, sick, sick!"

Everyone laughs except Mary Ann's mom. "I'm sure he's nice," she says.

"Time to say good-bye," my mom says.

Now I'm the one who feels sick. And I don't think it's from the M&Ms or the jelly beans on the pizza. I hug everybody, but I save Mary Ann for last.

When I hug her, she raises her pinkie on her right hand. "Let's pinkie swear." I hook my pinkie around hers.

"I pinkie swear I won't be friends with the boy next door," says Mary Ann.

Since I won't live here anymore, it doesn't make sense for me to pinkie swear that. But I have to promise something.

"I pinkie swear I'll never be friends with any boy next door."

Then we squeeze our pinkies together, and it's official.

I sure am going to miss Mary Ann.

WISH POND ROAD

I press a button on the side of my watch, and the face lights up. It's only 8:30 in the morning, and we've been driving for two hours.

I feel sick. The problem is I don't know if I'm carsick or moving sick. I clutch my stomach and lean over the front seat. "How much longer?" I moan.

"An hour," says Dad.

"Quiet," grumbles Max. He stretches and puts his feet on my side of the seat. "I'm trying to sleep."

I hold my nose and push Max's stinky feet back to his side of the car. I don't see how Max can even think about sleeping on a day like today.

We're moving, and my brain is filled with questions. I tap Dad on the shoulder. "Tell me why our street is named Wish Pond Road?"

Dad smiles at me in the rearview mirror. "Do you want to hear the Legend of the Wish Pond?"

Dad already told me this story, but I'm having a hard time deciding if I think it's true.

I shrug. I *don't* want Dad to get the wrong idea and think I'm excited about moving to a street named Wish Pond Road.

I *do* want to hear the story again.

Dad clears his throat. "Legend has it that many years ago, a farmer and his wife lived on a large and beautiful farm right where our street is now."

"What did they have on their farm?" I ask.

"Good question," says Dad. "They had just about everything a farmer and his wife could want. They had cows and pigs and chickens and goats. They had corn and

barley and wheat and hay.

"The only thing they didn't have that they wanted were children."

"How sad," says Mom.

"Yes," Dad says. "This made the farmer and his wife very sad indeed. Sometimes while the farmer was out tending to the cows and pigs and chickens and goats, the farmer's wife would go sit by herself on the edge of a small pond in the middle of the farm.

"One day she picked up a rock, threw it into the pond, and made a wish. *I wish I had a little boy or a little girl to sit next to me by this pond.*

"And to her amazement, her wish came true. The farmer's wife was blessed with a baby boy."

Max stretches across the backseat. "Lucky for her she got a boy."

I roll my eyes at Max. "I bet once he was old enough to talk she wished she could turn him into a girl."

"Quiet, you two, and let me finish the story," says Dad.

"The farmer's wife thought it was possible that her good fortune had come from throwing the rock into the pond," continues Dad. "So she threw another rock into the pond and again wished for a child. This time she and the farmer were blessed with a beautiful baby girl."

I grin at Max.

Dad keeps talking. "Now certain that the pond had magical powers, the farmer's wife decided to make one more wish. She threw another rock into the pond and this time, as was her wish, she was blessed with twins."

"Boys or girls?" I ask Dad.

"I don't really know," says Dad. "And I

don't think it matters. The story is that the farmer and his wife and their children lived long and happy lives on the farm."

"That was a long time ago," continues Dad. "Now the farm is gone, but the pond is still there. And those who know it believe it is a wish pond and that anyone who lives on this street can make three wishes, and they'll come true."

Dad stops his story. I sit quietly for a few minutes. There's something I've wanted to ask him since the first time I heard this story.

"Dad, how do you know the wish pond works?"

He smiles at me in the mirror. "I don't know if it works. We'll have to try it and see. But I think the question you have to ask yourself is if you believe in magic."

Cheeseburger stretches across my lap. I

hope the wish pond works. There are lots of things I've been wishing for lately. Like having someone to play with on our new street.

I rub Cheeseburger's back. "Hey, Dad, do any kids live on Wish Pond Road?"

"I saw some kids outside playing when I went to check on the house last week."

I cross my fingers. "Did you see any eight-year-old girls who looked like they didn't have a best friend?"

Max sits up. "Did any of them have wings and feathers and a head the size of a peanut? If so, they'd make a perfect friend for Mallory."

I glare at Max. "The first thing I'm going to do when we get to Wish Pond Road is throw a rock in the wish pond and wish for a different brother."

Max takes a doughnut out of a bag. He

shoves it in his mouth and gets crumbs all over his shirt. "You actually believe in magic?"

I look at the mess he's made. "So?"

Max shoves in another doughnut. "So, you would."

Now there are crumbs all over the backseat. "What's that supposed to mean?"

Max looks at me like he can't believe I don't know what he's talking about. "It means you're always doing dumb things, and believing in a magic wish pond is just another dumb thing."

"Max, be nice!" Mom gives him a *close-your-mouth* look.

But Max ignores it. "It's true," he says. "Remember when she tried to fly, and the whole neighborhood saw her do it?"

I'll never forget the day Mary Ann and I

tried to fly. We taped garbage bags to our arms and skated down the hill. Our plan was for the garbage bags to fill with air and lift us off the ground when we flapped our arms. Only too bad for us. . . the plan didn't work like we thought it would.

"Big deal," I say to Max. "I bet a lot of kids wish they could fly like birds."

"Yeah." Max pops another doughnut in his mouth. "But most kids know the difference between birds and humans."

I pick powdered sugar crumbs off my side of the seat. I bet most birds are neater eaters than my brother.

I lean over the seat and shake Mom's shoulder. "Hey, Mom, what's sitting in the backseat and looks like it got lost in a snowstorm?"

"What?" Mom turns around.

"Max! Messy Max!" I laugh so hard my

face hurts.

Mom tells Max to wipe his mouth and brush the powdered sugar off his shirt.

"Don't worry about me," says Max.

"Just look at the backseat," I say.

But Max looks right at me. "You messed up things in our old neighborhood. Try not to do it in the new neighborhood, too."

"I'm not going to mess up anything!" I shout.

"That's enough!" says Dad. He turns the car onto a small street.

A sign says Wish Pond Road. Neat rows of two-story white houses with green shutters and black front doors line both sides of the street.

Dad pulls the car into a driveway of a two-story white house with green shutters and a black front door. "We're here," he says. "Number 17 Wish Pond Road."

I get out of the car and look at my new house. It looks like all the other houses on the street.

I think about the farmer's wife and the pond and how her wishes came true. Then I close my eyes and make a wish.

I wish I didn't have to move into a white house with green shutters and a black door on a street called Wish Pond Road.

I hope my wish comes true. But if it doesn't, I hope I don't get confused and go into the wrong house.

THE GIRL NEXT DOOR

"Time for the official McDonald family tour," says Dad. He pushes open the front door to 17 Wish Pond Road, and we follow him inside.

First he shows us the family room.

Then the living room.

Then the dining room.

Then the laundry room.

I yawn. The only thing official about this tour is that it's officially boring.

"Now for the bedrooms," says Dad. He leads us into a bedroom downstairs.

"WOW!" Max and I say at the same time. This tour just got interesting!

This room's so big you could fit an elephant into it! I can't wait to call Mary Ann and tell her about my new room.

"Max, this is your room," says Dad. "Follow me. I'll show you Mallory's." We walk through a bathroom. "You two have to share," he says.

Max makes a face like he's going to puke. I don't want to share a bathroom with him either, but I can't wait to see my room.

Dad takes us into another bedroom. It looks like Max's room. But there's one big difference: It's tiny.

"This is a room for a mouse!" I say. "I want the other room."

"Taken," says Max.

"NO FAIR!" I stamp my foot. "Cheeseburger and I have to share a room. This one is too small for both of us."

"Too bad," says Max.

"Mom and I discussed it," says Dad. "It's the only fair way. Max is older."

"DAD!" I give him my *I'm-your-only-daughter* look. I nudge Cheeseburger to give him an *I'm-your-only-cat* look. But neither look does much good.

The doorbell rings. "End of conversation,"

says Dad. He walks out of my room, and I hear him greet the movers.

I look around my room. But it doesn't look like it belongs to me. It just looks like four white walls with none of my stuff on them.

I take my cat-of-the-month calendar out of my backpack and stick it on one of the walls with a pushpin. I pick up Cheeseburger. "Home, not-so-sweet home," I whisper in her ear.

We go outside and sit on the front porch. The movers are taking our stuff off the truck. Everything is wrapped in blankets so it doesn't even look like our stuff.

Then I get a horrible thought. What if it's not? What if the wrong moving truck showed up? What if we got somebody else's stuff, and they get all of ours?

I put my head down on Cheeseburger. I want to call Mary Ann. But what would I say?

Hi Mary Ann. Guess what? All the houses on my street look alike. I can't even tell which one is mine. My room is so small, I don't think there's enough air in there for Cheeseburger and me to make it through the night. And I'm probably going to have to wear some other kid's clothes because the wrong moving truck showed up with somebody else's stuff.

But I am so, so, so glad we moved.

I decide not to call Mary Ann yet.

A door slams and I jump. A girl in a bathing suit walks out of the house next door and into her front yard.

When she looks over, I wave.

She doesn't wave back. "Maybe she's shy," I whisper in Cheeseburger's ear.

She sits in a lawn chair, props her feet up on an ice chest, and puts on dark glasses and headphones.

The girl next door looks like a movie star. Maybe things on Wish Pond Road won't be so bad after all. I pick up Cheeseburger.

"Let's go introduce ourselves."

I walk up to her chair. "Hi," I say in my friendliest voice.

She doesn't move. Her music is probably so loud, she can't hear me.

I try again. Louder this time. "HI!"

She doesn't move. I tap her on the shoulder and use my outdoor voice. **"HI. I'M MALLORY. I'M MOVING IN NEXT DOOR. YOU CAN PROBABLY TELL BECAUSE OF THE MOVING TRUCK IN MY FRONT YARD."**

The girl next door takes off her glasses and looks at me. "You're in my sun."

I move to the other side of her chair. "Hey, hey, hey," I say. "I'm Mallory McDonald. Like the restaurant but no relation."

She takes her headphones off her ears. "Winnie Winston."

"Hey, that is so, so, so cool," I say. "Mallory McDonald. Double 'M'. Winnie Winston. Double 'W'. Get it?"

Winnie looks at me like I sneezed on her. "What I don't get is why you say everything three times? Is something wrong with you?"

I think for a second. I have six mosquito bites on my ankle. But other than that, I'm fine. I shake my head.

"Then why do you say things three times?" asks Winnie. "It's weird."

I start to tell Winnie it's not weird, it's my style. But I decide not to. I might decide to change my style.

"Are you eight?" I ask Winnie. "I'm eight."

Winnie stands up straight in front of me. She looks down at me, but she doesn't have to look too far. She's not much taller than I am. "Do I look like I'm eight?"

I look from the bottom of Winnie's feet to the top of her head. "Sort of. It's hard to tell."

Winnie stands up straighter. "I'm ten.

I'll be eleven in two weeks."

"My brother, Max, is turning eleven, too."

"Big deal." Winnie yawns. "Millions of kids are turning eleven."

I look at Winnie's bathing suit. "Were you going to swim in the wish pond? I can put on my bathing suit and go with you."

Winnie points to a pond at the end of our street. "First of all, that thing isn't a wish pond. Everybody knows it's just a plain old pond. And it's the last place I want to go swimming."

Winnie wraps her towel around her waist and looks at me. "Don't think we're going to be friends just because you live next door."

She puts her sunglasses on and walks back in her house. She doesn't even bother to pick up her chair.

I pick up Cheeseburger. *No problem.* I'll

just go see the wish pond myself.

I carry Cheeseburger to the end of my street. I love my cat, but I really wanted my first trip to the wish pond to be with a new friend.

I sit down with Cheeseburger on a big rock on the edge of the pond.

Maybe Winnie is right. Maybe it is just a plain old pond. But it looks like fun to get your feet wet in here.

I rub Cheeseburger's back. "What do you think of the girl next door?" I ask her. But Cheeseburger doesn't say a word.

I pick up a little rock on the edge of the pond and squeeze it in my hand. *I wish someone nice lived next door to me.* I throw my rock into the water.

I've met the girl next door, and I don't think there's much hope of that wish coming true.

JOKE JUICE

The calendar on my wall tells me something I don't want to know: I've lived here for two whole days, and I still don't have a friend. I sit down at my desk and scratch my head. Then I get out a pencil and make a list.

Things I Need to Make New Friends:
- 1 table
- 1 folding chair
- 1 pitcher of juice
- paper cups

First, I look for a table and folding chair. In my old house, I knew where to look for stuff. I have to look in three closets before I find what I need.

I set up the table and chair in our front yard.

Then, I go into the kitchen and get out a big pitcher. Time to make Joke Juice. The problem is, I've never made it before so I'm not sure what's in it.

I decide to use the 1-2-3-4-5 method.

One carton orange juice

Two cans grape soda

Three cups chocolate milk

Four teaspoons spaghetti sauce

Five drops blue food coloring

Salt

Pepper

Stir

I hold the pitcher up to the light and add

more spaghetti sauce. I hope Joke Juice tastes better than it looks.

I take the pitcher outside and put it on the table. Then I go to my room to make a sign. When I'm done, I read it to Cheeseburger.

I hurry outside, tape it to the front of the table, and sit down. All I have to do now is wait.

A boy rides over on a skateboard. A small black dog follows him. It sits when he snaps his fingers. "Hey, I'm Joey," he says. "I live next door."

I read his T-shirt.

I didn't do it, nobody saw me do it, I think I need to speak to my lawyer.

"I'm Mallory, and I've never met a kid who has his own lawyer."

"My grandpa gave me the shirt." Joey grins. "He's my lawyer, and he lives with me."

"You live with your grandpa?"

"And my dad and my sister."

"What about your mom?" I ask Joey.

Joey stops grinning. "She died. So my grandpa came to live with us."

I feel like someone punched me in the stomach. I don't know anyone whose mom died. I can't imagine what it would be like if my mom died.

"I'm sorry about your mom," I tell Joey.

"It's OK," he says. "It happened a long time ago."

"Is Winnie your big sister?"

"I don't like to tell people that when I first meet them," says Joey. "But we share the same gene pool. I'm not exactly what you'd call her favorite person."

"I know what you mean." I swat a mosquito off my face. "My brother, Max, feels the same way about me."

I point to Joey's dog. "Is he yours?"

Joey snaps his fingers. "Murphy, shake." Murphy holds up a paw, and I shake it.

I giggle. I'm not used to shaking paws with my neighbors. "How did he learn to shake?"

Joey rubs behind Murphy's ears. "Murphy can do lots of tricks." Joey claps his hands. Murphy lies down on the ground and rolls over.

"Wow!" I pick up Cheeseburger and introduce her to Joey. "I would tell her to shake, but she doesn't know how."

"Maybe we can teach her," says Joey.

Teaching Cheeseburger to do cat tricks sounds like fun. Then I remember my pinkie swear to Mary Ann: *I'll never be friends with any boy next door.* I don't say a word.

"What's Joke Juice?" Joey asks me.

I hold up the pitcher. Showing him how Joke Juice works does not exactly make us friends. "Gross!" he says.

"Magic!" I say. "When I drink it, I'll be able to tell a joke without having to think of one. Want to see?"

Joey nods.

I pour some Joke Juice into a cup. It smells like rotten tomatoes. Ugh! I close my eyes and take a sip. I hope I don't throw up.

I open my eyes and take a deep breath. "What does a raccoon get when it rains?"

"What?" asks Joey.

"Wet!"

"Good one." Joey laughs.

"Want to hear another one?" I take a sip of Joke Juice. I'm ready to tell my joke when Winnie walks over to my stand. "What's Joke Juice?"

I start to explain, but Winnie interrupts me. "Yeah, I can read. So let's hear a joke."

"How do you make a Dalmatian disappear?"

Winnie puts her hands on her hips. "How?"

"Spot remover!"

"Great joke!" Joey slaps his forehead.

Winnie rolls her eyes. "First of all, that's not what you use

spot remover for. And second of all, you don't need special juice to tell a joke that dumb."

My stomach feels funny. Maybe it's from the Joke Juice. "Watch again." I take another sip. "What do you call a stupid skeleton?"

"What?" asks Winnie.

"A bonehead."

Joey cracks up. Winnie stares at me. "Are you as good at spelling as you are at telling jokes?"

I'm a pretty good speller. I nod my head.

"Do you know what this word spells? B-O-R-I-N-G." Winnie stretches and pretends to yawn.

"What's going on?" Max comes outside and reads my sign.

"Do you know the amazing Mallory?" Winnie asks.

Max looks at Winnie like she's Miss America. Then he looks at me like I'm a leftover pickle. "I'm not in the mood for jokes," he says. He grabs my sign and my arm and drags me toward the front door.

"I'll be right back," I tell Joey and Winnie. "Careful with that sign," I tell Max. "I was just starting to make friends."

Max squeezes my arm. "Mom! Dad!" he yells when we're inside.

"What's wrong?" Mom rushes into the living room. Dad is right behind her.

"The Amazing Mallory has done it again." Max shoves my sign in Mom's face. "She's the laughingstock of Wish Pond Road and not because she tells funny jokes."

Mom and Dad read my sign.

Dad smiles.

"C'mon, Max," says Mom. "Mallory is just trying to make some new friends."

Max starts to say more, but I don't stay
to listen. I run into my room and slam the
door. I get it. The only joke here is me.

A PHONE CALL

"Which McDonald wants McDonald's tonight?" Dad grabs his car keys off the counter. He knows McDonald's is my favorite. I think he feels sorry for me because Max thought Joke Juice was a neighborhood joke.

"Last one in is a rotten egg," Dad says on his way out the door. Max is right behind him.

I try to catch up. But I can't. I have to waddle like a duck because my toenails are wet.

"Quack! Quack!" Max laughs as he passes me.

I ignore him. I don't want to mess up my polish.

On my way out the door, the phone rings. "I'll get it!" I waddle back over and pick it up.

"Hey, hey, hey!" says a voice on the other end.

It's Mary Ann! It's so great to hear her voice.

I plop down on the couch and wiggle my toes. They sparkle in the light. "Hey, hey, hey," I say.

"I have a surprise for you!" Mary Ann squeals so loudly I have to hold the phone away from my ear.

"Tell me! Tell me! Tell me!" I squeal back. I love surprises, and I'm going to pop if she doesn't spit this one out fast.

"I'M COMING TO VISIT!"

This is an amazing surprise.

"AWESOME! AWESOME! AWESOME!" I say. "We're going to have so much fun. We can even make a scrapbook of your visit."

I start to tell her all the fun things we can do when she's here. But I don't get too far.

"C'mon," Max yells from the front door. "We're waiting, and I'm starving."

I ignore Max. All he ever thinks about is baseball and what he's going to put in his stomach.

"When are you coming?" I ask Mary Ann. I don't think I can wait another day.

"In one month," she says. "Mom said she will drive me down, and we can stay for the weekend. ONE WHOLE WEEKEND!" she says.

But all I can think is: ONE WHOLE MONTH!

This is not totally awesome. This is totally terrible. How am I going to wait one whole month for Mary Ann to come visit?

"Get a move on," Max shouts from the door.

"I have to go," I tell Mary Ann. "But I promise to write."

"I promise to write you back," says Mary Ann.

"Bye, bye, bye." I pretend to cry into the phone.

"Bye, bye, bye." Mary Ann pretends to cry back.

I announce my surprise when I get into the car. "Mary Ann is coming to visit!"

Mom and Dad smile at each other. They don't seem surprised at all. But Max seems real surprised.

"Birdbrain is coming to Fern Falls!" He rolls down his window and leans his head out. "Help, I need air."

"Max!" Mom gives him a *don't-get-started* look. Dad points to a baseball field. "That's where you're going to play," he tells Max.

Now Max is more interested in talking about baseball than Mary Ann's visit. But her visit is all I can think about. I'm going to cross the days off my cat calendar until she gets here. I really miss not having a best friend on my street.

We get in line to order at McDonald's. When it's my turn, I don't even hear the lady ask what I want.

"Earth to Mallory," says Max.

I order a Happy Meal and sit down. But my mind is definitely not on food.

Max sits down across from me. He has a Big Mac, a large order of fries, and a chocolate milk shake on his tray.

I watch him dip two French fries in his

milk shake. He stuffs them in his mouth. *Disgusting!* Even though my brain is busy planning my weekend with Mary Ann, watching Max makes me think of a joke.

"What's as long as California and wider than Texas?" I ask.

Max doesn't say *what* like he's supposed to. I give the answer anyway. "Your stomach! Get it?"

"Here's a question for you," Max says without laughing. "What's the only good thing about all the dumb stuff you do?"

I take a bite out of my cheeseburger and ignore Max.

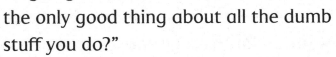

"We get to eat at McDonald's!" Max cracks up.

"Not funny," I say.

"News flash," says Max. "None of the dumb stuff you do is funny. So if you don't mind, lay off. I don't want the neighbors to think I have a total moron for a sister."

"Here's a news flash for you," I say to Max. "You're the only moron on our street." I take a sip of my Coke.

"Actually," I say to Max. "I don't know if you noticed, but the girl next door is a pretty big moron too."

Max sips his shake.

I stare at him. Max never sips his shake. He guzzles shakes. He slurps shakes. But he never ever sips them. That's when I get it: Max doesn't think the girl next door is a moron at all.

"You like Winnie!" I say. Now it's my

turn to crack up. This is even funnier than the jokes on my Happy Meal box.

"She's better than her brother," says Max. "Talk about a dumb kid."

"He's not dumb," I say. "He thought my jokes were hilarious."

"Shows what he knows." Max gets up to dump his tray in the trash.

Maybe Max is right about Joey. Maybe he's not. But it doesn't matter anyway. Mary Ann and I made a pinkie swear: *Never be friends with any boy next door.*

When I get home, I cross today off my calendar with a fat red marker. I draw a purple heart on the day Mary Ann is coming.

Just one month to go.

AN INVITATION

Ding-dong.

Ding-dong.

"Somebody get the door!" Dad shouts from upstairs.

I hop off the couch. It's our first official visitor, and I want to be the official greeter. I fling open the door.

Big mistake! It's Winnie with four things: a scowl on her face, Joey, and two bald guys.

Maybe Joey and the bald guys dragged

Winnie over to apologize to me. I saw a movie once where that happened.

The older bald guy hands me a bag. "Special delivery," he says.

What if there's something awful in the bag like a dead snake or a rat?

But I can tell by the smell it's not a dead snake or a rat. I open the bag and peek inside. Fresh hot bagels. Mmmm. I pick one and take a bite out of it. Double mmmm.

The younger bald guy talks first. "Hello, young lady," he says. "You've met my kids. I'm Winnie and Joey's dad, Mr. Winston, and this is my dad, Mr. Winston."

The older bald guy smiles. "You can call me Grandpa. Everybody does."

I take another bite out of my bagel. "I'm Mallory."

"Pleased to meet you, Mallory." Grandpa

shakes my bagel-free hand.

Mom comes up behind me and takes the bagel bag. "Mallory, don't be rude. Invite our guests in."

Dad comes downstairs, and the introductions start all over again.

Mr. Winston says he's sorry he hasn't come over sooner. Mom says we've been busy unpacking. Blah, blah, blah. For grown-ups who don't know each other, they have a lot to talk about.

Mom invites both Mr. Winstons in for coffee. Then she tells us kids to go play.

But we just stand there and look at each other. Don't grown-ups know that's what happens when they tell kids who don't know each other to go play?

"I'm going home," says Winnie. "I'm too old to

play." The front door slams behind her.

"Count me out." Max plops down on the couch. "I've got to do something really important, like finish this comic book."

That leaves Joey and me. I don't want to be friendly. But I don't want to be rude either. I take a bite out of my bagel.

"Want to see my room?"

"Lead the way," says Joey.

He follows me down the hall. It's hard to walk into my room because my scrapbooks are all over the floor. I push them into a pile in the corner to make room for both of us.

"It's a mess," I tell Joey. "We moved in

three days ago, and Mom says I have to have everything put away by the end of the week."

"No sweat," says Joey. "We moved in five years ago, and I still haven't finished putting my stuff away."

I think about Joey's mom. I wonder if Joey hasn't put his stuff away because he doesn't have a mom to tell him to do stuff like that. I feel bad just thinking about it.

But Joey doesn't look like he feels bad. He opens one of the joke books on my dresser. "What's another name for funny candy?" he asks.

I scratch my head. "I give up."

"Laughy taffy!"

"Ha-ha."

Joey closes the book. "You like jokes, don't you?"

"I used to," I tell him.

Joey looks at me like he's studying a long spelling word. "Were you upset the other day because Winnie didn't laugh at your jokes?"

Joey's pretty smart . . . for a boy.

"Yeah," I tell him. "I was a little mad at Winnie. But I was a lot mad at Max. He says everything I do is dumb."

"Your brother and my sister are going to get along great. Winnie thinks everything I do is dumb, too." Joey puts the joke book down. "It stinks, doesn't it?"

I roll my eyes. "Yeah, well what can we do?" Maybe no one's ever told Joey that big brothers and sisters get away with just about everything.

"We could give them a taste of their own medicine." He whispers like somebody is listening outside my door. "Play a joke on them. Something funny."

I look through my bookshelves. "Sorry," I tell him. "I can't find my copy of *Jokes to Play on Your Older Sibling*."

Joey grins. "We don't need a book. We'll think up our own joke."

"Like what?" I can't imagine what we could do to Max and Winnie.

"Joey. . . . " His dad calls him from the other room. "We're leaving."

"To be continued," says Joey.

When we walk back into the den, the grown-ups are saying good-bye. "See you tonight," Mr. Winston says to Mom as he leaves.

"Seven sharp," says Grandpa Winston.

Dad waves and closes the door behind them.

"Where are we going at seven sharp?" I ask Mom.

"To the Winston's." Mom opens a

box marked Cookbooks. "We've been invited to a v barbecue. I have to think of something to bring."

"I know what you can leave at home," Max mumbles from behind his comic book.

Mom doesn't hear him. But I do. I know he means me, *and* I know he thinks I'm going to do something to embarrass him, *and* I don't care.

I've been invited to a party!

I'm going to make a scrapbook of my move to Fern Falls. I'm going to call it *My Moving Book.* It will be like my baby book and the first picture in it will be from tonight. On the top of the page, I'm going to write: *Me at my first party in the new neighborhood.*

I just hope when I'm a grown-up and I look back at *My Moving Book,* I'll be smiling in the first picture.

THE "NO JOKE" CLUB

Whenever I'm waiting for someone to open a door, I wonder if I have a booger in my nose. I try to think about other things, but my brain only lets me think about what might be in my nose.

The good news is I've never actually had a booger while I'm waiting.

The bad news is I feel like I do today. I bet Winnie answers her front door, sees it, and laughs so hard her head falls off.

But I get lucky. Joey answers the front door, and he doesn't even look at my nose. He just looks happy to see us. "Come in," he says. "We've been waiting for you."

We follow Joey into the backyard. Winnie is sitting in a chair reading a magazine. She doesn't even get up to say hello.

Mr. Winston and Grandpa come over to greet us. "Hey!" says Mr. Winston. He twirls the chef's hat on his head. "I hope you like chicken."

Mom and Dad tell Mr. Winston they love it.

I tell Mr. Winston I love chicken jokes.

"Chicken jokes, huh." Mr. Winston smiles. "I'd love to hear a chicken joke."

Max gives me one of his *don't-do-it* looks.

I ignore him. "Why did the chicken cross the road?"

"That's the oldest, dumbest joke on the planet," Winnie says without looking up from her magazine.

"To get to the other side." I ask the next joke before anyone has a chance not to laugh at my first one. "Does anybody know why the rooster crossed the road?"

"Why?" Joey asks.

"To show he wasn't a chicken."

Everybody laughs. Well . . . almost everybody. Winnie yawns, and Max doesn't move a muscle. I'm starting to think the best way to keep Max quiet is to keep him with Winnie. He doesn't say a word when she's around.

The grown-ups start talking.

"Want to see my room?" Joey asks me.

"Sure." I follow him through his house. I thought it would be a big mess. But I'm surprised. It's pretty neat.

We pass one room that's very neat. It's also very pink. I know without asking who it belongs to.

"I'm dead meat if I go in there," Joey tells me.

That doesn't surprise me a bit. I bet the president of the United States would need an invitation to go into Winnie's room.

Then we go into Joey's room. At least we try to. There's stuff everywhere. "Sit anywhere you can find a spot," Joey tells me.

I move a pile of T-shirts off a beanbag chair and sit down.

Joey sits on the floor. "Dad says I have to clean my room by the end of the summer, or I have to repeat second grade."

"Is he serious?" I can't believe a parent would say that.

Joey grins. "My dad loves to joke around. Me too. Speaking of jokes, I thought of a joke we can play on Winnie and Max."

"Huh?" I say. I can't believe he's serious.

Joey puts his finger to his lips and sticks his head out his door. He looks up and down the hall. "Want to hear my plan?" he asks softly.

I nod. Joey sits on the pile of T-shirts on the floor and whispers his plan to me. I know no one can hear because he's whispering so softly I can barely hear him.

When he finishes, I can't believe what I heard. I thought it would be impossible to think of something to do to Winnie and Max, but Joey's plan is great.

"We'll start a club," he says. "The 'No Joke' Club."

I frown. That sounds like the wrong name for this club to me. "Aren't we going to play jokes on Max and Winnie?"

"Sure," Joey says. "But we have to show them that treating us nice is NO joke."

I smile. "I get it."

"Joey. Mallory." Joey's dad calls us from the backyard. "Time for dinner."

"So when do we put our plan into action?" I ask Joey.

"We start tomorrow." He high-fives me. The "No Joke" Club is official.

We go outside in the backyard. Mr. Winston gives everyone big plates of barbecued chicken and baked beans.

I take a bite of chicken. Mmmm. "What do you call chicken that tastes good?"

"I hope delicious," says Mr. Winston.

"Finger lickin' chicken!" I take a bite and lick my lips.

"I'm glad you like it." Mr. Winston smiles.

Winnie rolls her eyes, and Max doesn't even look up from his plate. I know he thinks my joke is funny because I've heard him laugh when I've told it before.

But I also know he isn't planning to laugh today. Max must have a rule about it: absolutely no laughing or talking around Winnie.

While Mr. Winston clears the chicken plates, I make a note in my head: *tell Max he should find a better way to show girls he likes them.*

Mom cuts the cake she brought. Everyone eats a piece, and then we go home.

When I get in my room, I turn out my light and get right in bed.

Life on Wish Pond Road might not be so bad after all.

PAINTED
TOENAILS

I count red Xs on my calendar and force myself to do some math, even though it's summer break. The results are worse than I thought they would be.

It's been exactly two weeks, two days, fourteen hours, and twenty-two minutes since I promised Mary Ann I would write her a letter.

And I am going to write her. The problem is for the past two weeks, two days, fourteen hours, and twenty-two minutes, I've been very, very, very busy.

And I'm still very, very, very busy. I'm supposed to be at the wish pond this very minute for morning cat tricks.

I grab doughnuts with one hand and Cheeseburger with the other.

"C'mon!" Joey waves when he sees me coming down the street. "Cat trick lessons start promptly at nine."

I plop down on the rocks beside the wish pond and hand Joey a doughnut. He's very serious about cat trick lessons.

I am too. But so far, Cheeseburger doesn't seem to be much of a student. Last week, we tried to teach her how to shake paws. Once, she shook her tail. But she never even lifted a paw.

This week we are trying to teach her to roll over.

"OK," Joey says to Cheeseburger. "Watch Murphy." He holds the doughnut in the air in front of Murphy.

"Murphy, roll over." Murphy rolls over, and Joey gives him a little piece of a doughnut. I clap. "Your turn," he says to Cheeseburger.

Joey holds up a little piece of doughnut. Cheeseburger closes her eyes and stretches out on the rock.

"Maybe she's not in the mood for doughnuts," I say.

"We can't give up," says Joey. He claps his hands, and Murphy rolls over again.

"C'mon, Cheeseburger," says Joey. But Cheeseburger won't even open her eyes.

We spend the morning trying to keep Cheeseburger awake. I take my shoes off and stick my feet in the wish pond. It's getting hot out here.

Joey takes his shoes off too. "Maybe we should try again this afternoon after we skateboard."

Yikes. Joey and I always skateboard in the afternoons.

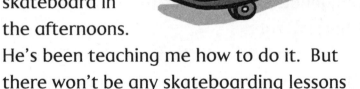

He's been teaching me how to do it. But there won't be any skateboarding lessons for me today.

I tell Joey there's something I *have* to do.

When I get home, I shut my door and sit down at my desk. I write Dear Mary Ann on the top of a piece of paper.

Then I just sit at my desk. Writing letters is not as much fun as skateboarding.

But I have to write something. I promised Mary Ann I would. The question is what.

I take out another sheet of paper and start over.

Dear Mary Ann,

I have something to tell you that I think you will like hearing. You know what a pain Max is, right?

Joey (my next-door neighbor) helped me play a really funny trick on him. We snuck into Max's room while he was still sleeping and painted his toenails.

Can you believe it?

I did the actual painting while Joey held his hand over my mouth. When we finished, we crept back into my room and burst out laughing. Max looked so funny.

When he woke up, he went nuts. (You know how nuts he can be.)

He was screaming and yelling. "GET THIS STUFF OFF OF ME! MALLORY, I'm GOING TO KILL YOU!"

He was hopping up and down and trying to wipe his toenails on my carpet. When he saw Joey (who he calls Kangaroo Boy, because he says a joey is the official name for a baby kangaroo), he yelled at him to hop back into his pouch.

You should have seen Max with sparkly purple toes. It was so funny!

We played a trick on Joey's sister (who is not nice . . . AT ALL!) too. One morning, Joey and I went into Winnie's bathroom while she was sleeping. We lifted up the toilet seat and stretched plastic wrap tight across the toilet. Then we put the seat down.

We hid in Joey's room and waited until we heard Winnie go into the bathroom.

When we heard her scream, we knew what had happened. Winnie came out of the bathroom, carrying her slippers. They were dripping wet with you-know-what. You should try this sometime (not to yourself, to someone else). It is so, so, so funny!

I can't wait for you to get here. G.2.G. (short for got to go). I'm late for skateboarding lessons.

Hugs and Kisses!
Mallory

I reread my letter. In second grade, I learned there are three steps to writing a letter.

Step 1: Writing it.
Check.
Step 2: Rereading it.
Check.
Step 3: Mailing it.
There's no way I can do step three!
Joey and I have had a lot of fun since I moved in. But I think about the pinkie swear I made with Mary Ann. *I promise not to be friends with any boy next door.*

When Mary Ann reads my letter, she'll know I broke my pinkie swear. She won't be happy about that.

I don't know how I'm going to tell her I'm friends with Joey, but I do know writing it in a letter is a bad idea.

I rip up my letter. Then I look in my mirror and raise my right hand.

Tomorrow, I do solemnly swear to write Mary Ann.

A BAD MONTH

Dear Mary Ann,

I don't think letters are supposed to have titles. But if they did, I'd call this one A Bad Month.

Lots of bad things have happened since I moved to Fern Falls. I will tell you about them all.

Bad thing #1: My room is very, very, very small. Max got the big room, and I got the very, very, very small room.

Bad thing #2: My bathroom is not

actually my bathroom. It is the bathroom I have to share with Max. (You'll have to share with him, too, when you come visit. But don't worry, we can lock him out. Maybe we'll lock him out all day, and if he has to go really bad, he'll have to go in the backyard. Ha! Ha! Ha!)

Bad thing #3: My next door neighbor is a very mean girl. VERY, VERY, VERY MEAN! The only person who likes her is Max (so you can imagine how mean she must be). She doesn't even talk to me except to tell me to leave her alone. YOU WON'T LIKE HER.

Bad thing #4: There's a wish pond on my street, but I don't think it works. Wishes are supposed to come true when you throw rocks into the pond. But I've been throwing them in since I moved here, and none of my wishes have come true. If they had, I would still be living next door to you.

That's all there is to tell about me. Everything was bad when I moved in a month ago, and it hasn't gotten any better since.

I can't wait to see you. We're going to have so, so, so much fun. It will be just like it used to be.

We'll paint our toenails. We'll take Cheeseburger on long walks. We'll say

everything three times. We'll even play our favorite game (you know which one that is)!

I miss you so, so, so much! I am counting the days until you get here! (max says he is too.)

Hugs! Hugs! Hugs! Kisses! Kisses! Kisses!

mallory

I reread my letter. Even though I don't love, love, love writing letters, I think this one is good. I told Mary Ann about all the bad things that have happened to me since I moved here.

Then I think about what I *didn't* tell her. I didn't tell her that even though we made a pinkie swear not to be friends with the boy next door, I am.

I wrote in my letter that things will be just like they used to be. But I'm not sure how things with Mary Ann will be just like they used to be because now I'm friends with Joey, too.

All this thinking has given me a headache. I know why I don't like writing letters. You have to think about what you write in them, and I'm sick of thinking about what I've written in this one.

I put the letter to Mary Ann inside a purple envelope and lick it shut. I write S.W.A.K on the outside with a purple marker.

My letter to Mary Ann is sealed with a kiss, and it is on its way.

MALLORY IN THE MIDDLE

Dear Mallory,

I got your letter. I can't wait to see you!

I'm not writing much.

I'm going to see you so, so, so soon and we can talk, talk, talk then.

We're going to have so much fun!

No one to bug us (except Max, of course!).

Just you and me. Just like old times.

Hugs! Hugs! Hugs! Kisses! Kisses! Kisses!

Mary Ann

There are three good reasons not to hide inside a curtain:

One. It's itchy.

Two. It's stinky.

Three. It's hard to read your mail.

I don't actually know why I'm trying to read Mary Ann's letter. I've read it so many times I've practically memorized it.

Especially the part about *just you and me, just like old times.*

When I lived next door to Mary Ann, it was just the two of us. But now I live next door to Joey. If I add up Mallory plus Mary Ann plus Joey, I get three.

And the bad thing about the number three is that someone is always in the middle. And I feel like that someone is going to be me.

I bend down to scratch my foot, but someone gets to it before I do.

"Gotcha!" Max pulls me out of my hiding spot. "How come you're not outside with Kangaroo Boy waiting for Birdbrain?"

Max laughs. "Those two animals should get along great."

I never talk to Max about my problems, but I could use some advice right now. "That's the problem," I tell him. "I haven't told Mary Ann I live next door to a boy who's my new friend. And I haven't told Joey my old best friend is coming to visit."

I look at Max. I hope he'll tell me what to do. And he does.

"Better get back inside those curtains."

Max laughs. "You're toast."

A car honks. Max is right. I am toast. Burned toast with no butter or jelly.

"C'mon." Max pulls me outside. "This visit might actually be fun."

I shove Mary Ann's letter in my pocket and run outside. Somehow I have to keep Mary Ann and Joey apart.

"MALLORY!" She runs to hug me. "I am so, so, so happy I'm here!"

I'm happy she's here too. I'm also happy Joey isn't outside in his front yard.

Our moms hug. Mary Ann's mom takes my mom by the arm, and they start walking into my house. "You have to show me absolutely everything," she says.

Mary Ann takes my arm. "Me too," she says. "I want to see everything."

"Mallory has a lot to show you," says Max.

I roll my eyes at him. He could probably get in the *Guinness Book of World Records* for Worst Older Brother.

"Wish pond first," says Mary Ann.

Mary Ann is usually full of good ideas, but this isn't one of them. If Joey sees us outside, he'll come too. I've got to keep Mary Ann inside.

I pull her by the hand. "House first."

I give her a tour of my room.

Then my house.

Then the closets in my house.

I want this tour to take as long as possible.

"Now for the kitchen drawers," I say. "You need to know where we keep the spoons in case you need a midnight snack and I'm asleep."

Mary Ann yawns. "This is boring. Let's go outside."

I've got to keep Mary Ann inside. I drag her back to my room. "There's something we have to do . . . it's toe time!" I sit down on the floor and start painting.

Mary Ann sits down and paints her toes too. As soon as all ten of hers are purple and shiny, she screws the top back on the bottle of polish. She stands up and slips on her flip-flops. "C'mon, I want to see the wish pond."

I put my toes carefully through the

fronts of my flip-flops. "Not so fast," I tell Mary Ann. "You don't want to mess up your polish."

I have a bad feeling about what she's going to find at the wish pond.

"Show me how it works," Mary Ann says when we get there. "I want to make a wish."

I pick up two rocks and hand one to Mary Ann. I want to make a wish too. But the moment I haven't been waiting for happens before I have a chance to wish it doesn't.

Joey walks out of his house and over to the wish pond.

"Hey, Mallory." Joey talks to me, but he's looking at Mary Ann. "Who's this? I've never seen her before."

I throw in my rock and make a quick wish. *I wish old friends and new friends can*

become instant friends.

I introduce my friends to each other. "Joey. Mary Ann. Mary Ann. Joey." I feel like they should shake.

"Mallory and I are best friends." Mary Ann smiles at Joey. "I'm visiting her for the weekend."

"Really?" Joey scratches his head like he's confused.

"Yes, really," says Mary Ann. "And we're going to have a great, great, great time because we're best, best, best friends. We lived next door to each other all our lives. Until she moved here, of course."

"Hmmm." Joey says *hmmm* like he's in math class trying to think of an answer he really doesn't know. "That's weird."

Mary Ann rolls her eyes. "What's so weird about that?"

Joey picks up a rock and throws it across

the pond. "It's weird that Mallory never told me you were coming to visit. I live next door to her. We play together every day, and she's never told me about you. I'm surprised. That's all."

I try to speak. But it's kind of hard when it feels like you've got a giant wad of gum stuck in your throat.

Mary Ann looks confused. "Who is this kid?"

I cross my freshly painted toes. I hope she understands.

I whisper in Mary Ann's ear so Joey can't hear me. "Even though we pinkie swore we wouldn't be friends with a boy next door, I have to play with Joey because I don't have anybody else to play with."

Mary Ann smiles. She looks like what I said makes sense to her.

Then I look at Joey. Max always tells me

boys don't care about secrets. But Joey looks like he cares about the one I just whispered to Mary Ann.

I lean over and whisper in Joey's ear. "Mary Ann rode in a car for three hours to come see me. While she's here, I have to play with her. But when she leaves, we'll play. OK?"

Joey picks up a rock and throws it across the pond. "No," he says. "Not OK. Why can't we all play?"

How do I tell Joey that's a bad idea? Some people say having two friends means double the fun. But I'm beginning to think it means double the trouble.

"What a great idea!" says Mary Ann. Joey can play with us."

Did I hear her right? Did Mary Ann say Joey can play with us?

"Cool," says Joey.

Cool is right. I know why Mary Ann has been my best friend since I was born.

"So what are we going to play?" Joey asks.

"Mallory and I are going to teach you how to play our favorite game."

"Mega cool," says Joey. "I can't wait."

But I groan. This is not mega cool at all. I know the game we're going to play. It's my favorite game, and it's Mary Ann's favorite game.

But I don't think Joey's going to like it at all.

TASTER'S
CHOICE

"OK," says Mary Ann. "Here's how you play."

She goes in the pantry and gets down boxes and bottles and jars. She goes to the refrigerator and brings out bowls and pitchers and plates.

When Mary Ann is finished, our kitchen table is covered with eggs, olives, peanut butter, pickles, sardines, gooseberry jelly, black licorice, biscuit dough, flour, butter, marshmallows, baking soda, lemon juice, leftover meat loaf, tuna fish, an onion, eggplant casserole, shredded coconut, frozen peas, coffee creamer, and prune juice.

Ick. When I look at some of the stuff on the table, I'm not sure why Mary Ann and I like this game. But we do.

In second grade, we played until we tasted everything in the kitchen. We even tasted some things from the bathroom like hand lotion and hair conditioner.

"Mallory, since you know how to play, you're first." Mary Ann takes the bandanna off her head and ties it around my eyes.

Then she explains the rules to Joey. "I'm going to spin Mallory around three times. Then she points to something on the table. Whatever she chooses, she has to taste. Then she has to guess what it is. Get it?"

"Got it," says Joey. "But what if you don't like what you taste?"

"Too bad," says Mary Ann. "That's how you play."

"OK," says Joey. "It can't be that bad. Right?"

"Right." Mary Ann giggles.

Wrong, I think to myself. I don't like the sound of Mary Ann's giggle.

She checks my blindfold and spins me. When I stop spinning, I point. I can't see, but I hear Mary Ann and Joey laughing. Not a good sign.

"Open up," says Mary Ann. She puts something cold and squishy in my mouth.

Ugh. Disgusting!

"Chew," Mary Ann says. "You know the rule." I do know the rule. *You have to eat the whole bite.* I wish I could spit this out though. I don't like cold, squishy foods.

"What is it?" asks Mary Ann.

It's not a marshmallow. It's not a sardine. "Eggplant casserole?" I guess.

"Right!" Mary Ann and Joey laugh. I rip off the blindfold and gulp down a glass of water. Whoever made up the recipe for eggplant casserole made a big mistake.

Mary Ann is next. She gets baking soda.

My Aunt Sally used to put baking soda on my cousin Caroline when she had diaper rash. Anything that cures diaper rash must taste even worse than eggplant.

When it's Joey's turn, he gets frozen peas.

"Cold," he says after he makes his guess.

"But not too bad."

We play until we taste almost everything on the table. I get some really gross stuff. Flour, biscuit dough, and butter.

"Knock, knock," I say when I get butter.

"Who's there?" Mary Ann asks.

"Butter."

"Butter who?"

"Butter hope you get something that tastes better than butter."

Mary Ann laughs at my joke, but she doesn't get anything better. She gets some of the worst foods on the table. Prune juice, an onion, and leftover meat loaf.

Joey gets a marshmallow, peanut butter,

and black licorice. It's time to stop this game before someone gets something really gross. "Who wants to play outside?" I ask.

"One more round," says Mary Ann.

"OK by me," says Joey.

I don't know if it's the butter, the biscuit dough, or the idea of another round, but my stomach hurts. The blindfold goes back on. I get gooseberry jelly.

Mary Ann gets lemon juice.

When it's Joey's turn, Mary Ann blindfolds him and spins him really fast. When he points, his finger misses the table and points to something in the pantry.

The something

he's pointing to is Cheeseburger's cat food. Mary Ann covers her mouth to keep from laughing and takes a pellet out of the bag.

"NO!" I mouth to Mary Ann. But she pops the pellet in Joey's mouth before I can stop her. I cover my eyes. This is exactly what I didn't want to happen.

Joey chews. "UGH! DOUBLE UGH! TRIPLE, QUADRUPLE UGH!" He runs to the sink and spits. "It tastes like crunchy tuna fish."

"Guess again." Mary Ann starts laughing.

Joey rips the blindfold off. "I don't know what it is, but I'm going to be sick." He drinks straight from the faucet. "What was that?"

Mary Ann holds up the bag of cat food.

Joey stares at her. "You fed me cat food?"

Mary Ann is on the floor, she's laughing

so hard. I don't make a sound. I don't want Joey to think I had anything to do with this.

But Joey looks right at me. "How could you let me eat cat food?"

I try to explain that he pointed to it. That's how you play the game. That Mary Ann fed it to him . . . not me!

But the flour I ate must have turned into glue because my mouth is stuck shut.

"I thought you were my friend. Friends don't let friends eat cat food." Joey spits in the sink again. He stares at me. "I wish you didn't live next door to me!"

"Maybe your wish will come true," says Mary Ann.

But Joey doesn't stick around to find out how. The back door slams behind him.

Somehow, I knew this was going to be trouble. Part of me feels like I should run

after Joey and part of me feels like I want
to stay here with Mary Ann.

All of me feels like the cream filling
inside an Oreo must feel when the cookie is
pulled apart.

Two sides want me, and I don't know
who to stick to.

MALLORY IN A BOX

I never thought I wanted to see another box. But now I'm inside one on the way to Mary Ann's house, and no one even knows I'm gone.

I think back to Friday afternoon.

Mary Ann and I were in the kitchen trying to scrape dried biscuit dough off the counter when she told me her plan.

"NO WAY!" I shouted. "It'll never work."

"Of course it will." Then she got a piece

of paper and made a list of all the reasons
I should come live with her.

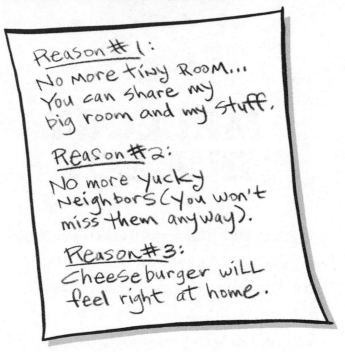

Reason #1:
No more tiny Room...
You can share my
big room and my stuff.

Reason #2:
No more yucky
Neighbors (you won't
miss them anyway).

Reason #3:
Cheeseburger will
feel right at home.

I read her list. Then I made my own list,
in my head, of all the reasons I should stay
where I am.

Reason #1: My room is tiny, but it has all
my stuff in it.

Reason #2: Only one of my neighbors is yucky (I will miss the other one).

Reason #3: Cheeseburger will miss her cat trick lessons.

I spent the whole weekend telling Mary Ann why her plan wouldn't work.

She spent the whole weekend trying to convince me that it would.

We were still in our sleeping bags this morning, and Mary Ann was still trying to get me to go along with what she had in mind.

"It's simple," she said for the ten-millionth time. "There's an empty box in the back of the van. When it's time for us to leave, just make sure no one is looking, and get in it. That's all you have to do."

"What happens when my mom and dad find out I'm gone?" I asked her for the ten-millionth time. "Then I'll be in trouble. BIG, BIG, BIG TROUBLE!"

"How can you get in trouble if they can't find you?" Mary Ann got out of her sleeping bag and sat on my dresser. She crossed her arms. "Anyway, you owe it to me. You broke your pinkie swear. You said you'd never be friends with any boy next door."

It made me mad that Mary Ann didn't understand that I didn't have a choice. "Who else was I going to play with?" I crossed my arms. "Max?"

Mary Ann thought for a minute. "Well, maybe you didn't have a choice," she said.

"It wasn't like you had me next door anymore. But now you do have a choice. You can follow my plan."

I didn't know what to say to that. Plus, riding in a box for three hours wasn't exactly my idea of fun.

"How do you know I'll fit in the box?" I asked Mary Ann.

"It's a big box," she said. "And once we get to my house, it'll be worth it. We'll be best friends like we used to be. Except even better because you'll be living with me."

Part of me wanted to go and part of me wanted to stay. I still wasn't sure which part I wanted to listen to, when Mary Ann said it was time to put our plan into action.

"Hurry!" she said. "I hear my mom telling your mom and dad good-bye."

"But I'm still in my pj's," I told Mary Ann.

She opened my window. "You've got to go now!"

And without another thought, I climbed out with Cheeseburger and got in the box in the van.

I could hear everyone come outside. I couldn't see, but I heard lots of good-byes and thank-yous.

Then I heard the words that made my heart beat so loudly I was sure someone would discover me.

"Where's Mallory?" asked Mom. "I know she'll want to say good-bye."

I thought I was toast for sure. But then Mary Ann said, "We already said good-bye. We stayed up all night talking. Mallory's taking a nap."

She whispered the part about the nap like she didn't want to wake me up.

Then Mom said I'd made a good choice,

and the next thing I knew, we were off.
Good-bye Wish Pond Road.

Hello box . . . hot, small, scratchy box.
I try to think of things I can do inside this
box for the next three hours.

But all I can think of are things I can't do.

I can't sing.

I can't sneeze.

I can't even go to the bathroom.

I try to think about all the fun Mary Ann
and I are going to have when we get to
her house, but my brain keeps thinking
about all the things I won't be able to do.

I won't be able to stick my feet in the
wish pond.

I won't be able to be in The "No Joke"
Club.

I won't even be able to fight with Max.

I can hear Mom's words. *I'd made a good
choice.*

Even though I really want to be with Mary Ann, I feel like I've made some not-so-good choices. Like leaving home in this box. Like letting Mary Ann feed Joey the cat food. I should have stopped her.

The more I think about it, the worse I feel. If I did to myself what I did to Joey, I wouldn't even be my own friend.

I bet that cat food tasted really gross. Just like the inside of this box smells.

I move my legs and try to get comfortable. But that's not so easy to do when you're cooped up inside a smelly box with nothing to do but think about your choices.

I look at my watch. Two hours and thirty-three minutes to go.

I remember what Mary Ann said. *Once we get to my house, it'll all be worth it.*

I hope she's right.

I look at Cheeseburger who is asleep on my lap. Nothing seems to be bothering her. Cats are lucky. They don't have to make choices.

Even though I wouldn't want to eat cat food, sometimes I think it would be a whole lot easier to be a cat.

NEVER COMING OUT

"I'm not going back, and you can't make me!"

Dad isn't listening to one word I've said. He might as well be dragging me by my hair like a cave girl.

I dig my heels into the gravel in Mary Ann's driveway. "I don't want to go back to Fern Falls!" I yell. "I want to stay here and live with Mary Ann."

At least . . . I think I do.

I had fun living with Mary Ann. Even if it was only for five hours and thirty-three minutes. We did a lot of things Mary Ann and I love to do. We ate cold pizza for lunch. We looked at old scrapbooks we made together. We made up a list of secret passwords in case we ever need them.

But there were a lot of things I like doing with Joey that I didn't get to do when I lived with Mary Ann . . . like going to the wish pond and skateboarding and playing with Murphy and Cheeseburger.

But still, I went to a lot of trouble to get here, and I'm not ready to go back yet.

I hold tight to Cheeseburger and hide behind Mary Ann. "We're not leaving!"

Dad reaches behind Mary Ann and grabs my arm. "I'm sorry," he says to Mary Ann's mom. "Get in the car young lady. You've got some explaining to do" is what he says to me.

As soon as I buckle my seat belt, Dad starts with questions.

Did I realize that I ran away from home?

Did I care that he and Mom were worried about me?

Did I think I could live at Mary Ann's house?

Did I know he would have to drive six hours to get me and bring me home?

Did I consider anyone's feelings other than my own?

I cross my arms. What about how I feel?

I felt weird when we got to Mary Ann's house and she said to me, "You're home." When I looked out her window at what used to be my home, it didn't look like my home anymore. It wasn't even the same color as it was when it was mine.

When Mary Ann and I were next-door neighbors, it was easy to be best friends. Now it's hard because everything is different.

"Earth to Mallory," Dad says. "I'm waiting for some answers."

But I have questions of my own.

"Why can't I live in one place with all the people I like and do all the things I like doing?" I kick the back of Dad's seat. "It's not fair."

Dad looks back at me in the mirror. His face is serious.

"Mallory, things change. I know moving hasn't been easy for you. But Mary Ann will

always be your friend. You don't live in the same place anymore, and it's important for both of you to make new friends."

This isn't what I want to hear. I wish Dad would say something like, *"Mallory, honey, we're sorry we ever made you move. We know this has been hard for you and we feel awful about it. We want to make it up to you somehow. We'll do anything. Even give away Max."*

But that's not what Dad says.

"Running away from home was wrong," says Dad. "We didn't know where you were. We looked everywhere. We were worried about you. We love you very much."

I cross my hands in my lap. Dad always says stuff like that when he's mad at me. It would make things a lot easier if he would say, *"Mallory, we hate you very much."* Then I could say, "I hate you very much" right back.

But now I don't know what to say. I scratch behind my ear. "I'm sorry," I mumble to Dad in the front seat.

"Apology accepted," says Dad. "I think we've cleared the air."

Not totally. There's one thing I still want to know. "Dad," I ask. "How did you know where I was?"

"Thankfully, Joey had the good sense to tell us he saw you get into the van."

My face feels hot. Did I hear Dad right? How could Joey tell on me?

"Joey did the right thing," says Dad. "I'm proud of him."

Proud of him? How can my Dad be proud of a rat?

Mary Ann should have fed him rat food, not cat food. When I see him, I'm going to feed him some. How could he give away my secret?

Dad and I ride the rest of the way without saying anything. I try counting trees to make the time pass. But I stop when I get to 1,062. I've spent a lot of time in a car lately, and this ride is making me sick.

Dad pulls into the driveway. "Home sweet home," he says. But I don't say a word. Part of me is kind of glad I'm back on Wish Pond Road. Part of me wishes I wasn't.

Mom and Max are waiting for me on the front porch.

"Too bad," says Max as I get out of the car. "I was just getting used to being an only child."

"Max, not today," says Mom. She tries to vhug me, but I run past her to my room. I slam my door and lay down on the bed.

I cover my head with my pillow. I want to be left alone, but I hear something.

Knock. Knock.

"Mallory, open the door."

I shove my fingers in my ears.

Knock. Knock. Knock.

"C'mon, Sweet Potato," says Mom.

"I'm not opening my door."

Knock. Knock. Knock. Knock. Knock.

"Go away! I don't feel like talking."

Mom and Dad whisper to each other. "Maybe we should leave her for a while," says Dad. "She knows what she did."

I hear them walking down the hall. I curl up on the bed next to Cheeseburger and stare out the window.

I'll leave with Cheeseburger. Mary Ann can come with us. We'll live at Disney World. We'll never go to school. We'll eat all the junk food we want. Nobody will be able to tell us what to do.

It's a lot to think about. I roll over and close my eyes.

When I hear a knock on my door, I rub my eyes and look outside. It's almost dark. I've been asleep for a while.

"Mallory," Mom says softly. "Dinnertime."

I turn on my light. Then I remember. "No

dinner for me." I lie back down on the bed.

"Knock, knock," says Mom.

I don't answer.

Mom tries again. "Knock, knock."

"Who's there?" I play along because I know Mom won't stop unless I do.

"Olive."

I know this joke. "Olive who?"

"Olive you," says Mom.

"I have a joke for you," I tell Mom.

"I would love to hear it," Mom says.

"What has red hair, freckles, and is really, really, really miserable?"

Mom doesn't say *what*. I open my door and finish my joke anyway.

"ME! I am really, really, really miserable. And I don't want

ME → (MiseRaBLe)

dinner. What I want is to make a wish, and I want it to come true."

Mom looks at me for a long time like I'm a tricky question on a crossword puzzle. "Mallory," she finally says. "Why don't you take a walk to the wish pond?"

"What for? If I throw in a million rocks, I don't think my wish will come true."

"Well, it certainly won't come true if you stay locked up in your room," Mom says.

"Fine, fine, fine." I walk out the door and head toward the wish pond.

But if my wish doesn't come true this time, I'm calling a wish pond repairman.

WISHES COMING TRUE

I sit down on the edge of the wish pond, pick up a rock, and throw it in. *I wish things never had to change.*

I dig my fingers through the rocks on the edge of the pond. There are red rocks and gray rocks and white rocks. There are big rocks and little rocks and flat rocks. There are lots of rocks, which is a good thing because I have lots of wishes.

Something catches my eye. It's a teeny,

tiny black pebble, but it's very shiny. When I pick it up, it feels warm and smooth in my hand. Something about this rock feels special.

I close my eyes. *I wish . . .*

But I don't finish. Someone sits down beside me.

"You're back," says Joey.

I open my eyes. "Thanks to you. Otherwise I would have been gone for good." I put my shiny black pebble on the ground and cross my arms.

"Hey, where did you find this?" Joey picks up my pebble.

"Give it back!" I grab it out of his fingers.

"It's yours," Joey says. "A wish pebble only works for the person who finds it."

A wish pebble. I've never heard of a wish pebble. I don't feel like having a conversation with Joey, but I want to know what he's talking about.

"What's a wish pebble?"

"You don't know?" Joey seems surprised. "Everyone on this street knows about wish pebbles."

"I haven't lived here that long. Remember?"

"These shiny black ones are wish pebbles," Joey says. They're rare and hard to find. I've searched through these rocks since I moved here and never found one. You're lucky."

I turn the pebble over. "What's so special about a wish pebble?"

Joey laughs. "When you make a wish with a wish pebble, your wish is supposed to come true."

I think about the Legend of the Wish Pond. Maybe the farmer's wife found three wish pebbles. This wish is important. I squeeze my pebble.

"Go ahead," says Joey. "Throw it in. But make sure you wish for what you really want."

"Shhh," I say. "I can't wish while you're talking."

I close my eyes. *I wish things never had to change.* I squeeze the pebble in the palm of my hand. I'm ready to throw my wish pebble in the pond.

"Know what?" Joey says.

I hold on to my pebble and open one eye. It's hard to make a wish when you're interrupted. "What now?"

"I'm glad you're back. When you left, I came down here and looked for a wish pebble. I tried to wish you back. But I couldn't find a wish pebble so that's why I told your parents."

Joey picks up a plain gray rock and throws it into the pond. "Wish Pond Road was no fun without you."

I close my eye. Even though I don't like that Joey told on me, I do like living on Wish Pond Road and being friends with Joey.

I squeeze the pebble in my hand. Then I change my wish.

I wish I could be friends with Mary Ann and Joey. I throw my wish pebble into the pond and wait for something to happen.

And it does. I get a feeling . . . a feeling that my pinkie swear doesn't matter anymore . . . a feeling that I can be friends with Mary Ann and Joey . . . a feeling that my wish is coming true.

I open my eyes and smile. "Hey, Joey, want to hear a joke?"

He nods.

"Knock, knock."

"Who's there?"

"Ima."

"Ima who?"

"Ima sorry I fed you cat food."

Now it's Joey's turn to smile. "That's OK. I kind of liked it. But next time, I'm going to try it with ketchup."

"DISGUSTING!" I lean over into the wish pond. "I think I'm going to puke!"

"Gotcha!" says Joey. "But next time we play, I go first."

"I don't know about that!" What I do know is that if I don't get home for dinner, I'll be in big trouble. And I've been in enough trouble for one day.

I open the front door and take a deep breath. Something smells terrific. I head straight for the kitchen. Mom, Dad, and Max are eating Chinese food.

I'm so hungry, I skip the chopsticks and pick up a fork.

Mom and Dad look at each other but don't say a thing. When I'm done, Max hands me a fortune cookie.

"I saved it for you," he says.

I open it and unroll my fortune. *No need to worry. Good times ahead for you on Wish Pond Road.*

There's something fishy about this fortune. I look at Max. He's trying not to smile.

I pop my cookie in my mouth. Then I
hand him the fortune. "You'll have to save
this for someone who needs it," I tell him.

I'm not worried a bit.

Dear Mary Ann,

How are you? I'm fine . . . NOW! But I wasn't when I left your house. Boy was I in big trouble. You should have heard Dad in the car. (Actually, you're lucky you didn't have to!)

He was VERY, VERY, VERY MAD that I ran away from home. I won't go into the whole thing, but the whole way home he was like Mallory this and Mallory that.

Mallory, Mallory, Mallory. Running away from home was wrong, wrong, wrong.

I wanted to explain to Dad that I knew running away from home was wrong. That you've always been my best friend. That I didn't want you to think I broke our pinkie swear.

But then Dad said, "Mallory, things change. Mary Ann will always be your friend. You don't live in the same place anymore, and it's important for both of you to make new friends."

And then I didn't say much. I didn't know what to say.

I went to the wish pond to wish that things never had to change. But I guess Dad is right. Things do change, and we both have to make new friends. It makes me sad that we can't live next door to each other and be best friends every day.

But I have a great, great, great idea. Next time you visit, we'll go to the wish pond and make a wish together.

We'll wish that one day we can live next door to each other.

Just think how much fun we'll have! We'll do everything together. We'll chew the same kind of gum. We'll paint our

toenails the same color, and we'll say
everything three times!
   Hugs! Hugs! Hugs!
   Kisses! Kisses! Kisses!
   mallory

   P.S. mom says you can visit again soon.
I asked, "How soon?" She said, "Very
soon!" And I said, "Unless it's tomorrow, it's
not soon enough for me!"
   P.P.S. Friends-4-ever-and-ever-and-
ever!

Back to School, Mallory

For Ellen Stein, editor extraordinaire...
and a fabulous friend
—L.F.

For Addison
—T.S.

Back to School, Mallory

illustrations by Tamara Schmitz

MINNEAPOLIS

CONTENTS

A WORD FROM MALLORY

My name is Mallory McDonald (like the restaurant, but no relation), age eight and almost 3/4. Until two months ago, my life was perfect. Nothing awful had ever happened to me.

Until my parents made me move to a new town. I had to get used to a new house, a new room and, worst of all, a new best friend. It was really, really, really hard.

Now my parents want me to start third grade at a new school. And guess what they want me to bring with me ... MY MOM!

When I found out she was hired to be the new music teacher at Fern Falls Elementary, I had what Dad calls a Mallory Meltdown (it sounds like an ice cream sundae, but trust me ... it's not!).

"Mom can't go to school with me!" I screamed. "Kids take notebooks and pencils and rulers and erasers to school, but they don't take their moms!"

Mom looked at me calmly. "Some kids do."

"But I don't want to be one of them!" I stamped my feet and shook my head. "It's hard enough being the new kid. I don't want to be the new kid who brings her mom with her!"

Mom just looked at me and shook her head.

"Please!" I begged. "Can't we at least talk about it?"

"Mallory," Mom said. "There's nothing to talk about. Come Monday morning, you and I are going to Fern Falls Elementary— TOGETHER!"

And that's when I got a feeling . . . a taking-my-mom-to-school-with-me-doesn't-seem-like-a-good-way-to-start-third-grade feeling.

I'm sunk. I'm doomed. I'm dead meat. And I haven't even started school yet.

A BAD START

Someone sits down on my bed and rubs my back. "Guess who?" says a voice.

Even though I'm covered with covers, I don't have to guess. I know it's Mom.

She tickles my back. "Rise and shine, Sleepyhead. Summer vacation is officially over." Then she whispers in my ear. "I have a back-to-school surprise for you. I'm making chocolate chip pancakes— your favorite!"

Mom always has a surprise for me on

the first day of school. I think she thinks that's what it takes to get me excited about going back to school. I usually am excited, but today is different.

"I have a surprise for you too," I tell Mom. I stick my hand out of the covers and hand her a sheet of paper. "Read!" I say.

Mom is quiet for a minute, and then she clears her throat and starts reading.

10 Reasons Why I, Mallory McDonald, Can NOT Go to School Today.

REASON #1: There are lots of germs at school. I could get sick.

REASON #2: The water fountain might explode, and I could get wet.

REASON #3: A big, fat, mean, ugly fifth grader might step on my toe and crush it.

REASON #4: I could get food poisoning if I eat lunch in the cafeteria.

REASON #5: It might snow, and school would be canceled anyway.

REASON #6: Max would like it better if I stayed home and so would Cheeseburger who will be one very, very, very lonely cat without me.

REASON #7: Someone should be home in case we get a delivery.

REASON #8: If I stay home, I will rake the front yard. (I promise!)

REASON #9: I'm pretty smart and probably don't need to go to third grade.

REASON #10: Even if I do, I want to be homeschooled.

Mom sighs. "Mallory, going to a new school is scary. And I know you're not happy I'm going with you, but if you'll give it a chance, I'm sure everything will work out fine."

She rubs my back through the covers. "You'll get used to the new school, and before you know it, you'll forget all about your old school."

"BRRNNNK!" I make a sound like a buzzer going off in a game show when the person on stage gets the answer wrong. "I'll never forget about my old school!"

Or my old best friend, Mary Ann. She has Mrs. Thompson this year.

Mrs. Thompson is the nicest third-grade teacher on the planet. She keeps a candy jar on her desk with a note taped to it: *"Take one if you're having a bad day."*

Mary Ann and I have been waiting since

kindergarten to have her, and now Mary Ann has her . . . without me. It's not fair! I pull my blanket in around me.

Mom tries to pull the covers off of me. "C'mon, Mallory, we both have to go to school. What do you say we start the year off right by being on time the first day?"

But there's only one thing I have to say: "I'M NOT GOING TO SCHOOL TODAY!"

Mom stops pulling. "Sweet Potato, I'm sure with Mrs. Daily as your teacher, today will be a good day." Mom chuckles. "In fact, I think with Mrs. Daily, good things will happen on a daily basis. Get the joke? Mrs. Daily. Daily basis."

I get it. And I love jokes, but lately, I haven't been in the mood. I don't move.

"C'mon," says Mom. "Joey's in your class. There's another good thing."

I'm happy Joey's in my class. We've had a lot of fun since I moved in next door to him. But I wish he could be in my class in my old school . . . not in a new school.

Mom pats my covered-up head. "Five minutes," she says in her *I-mean-business* voice. "I don't want your back-to-school surprise to get cold."

"OK, OK," I mumble. When Mom leaves, I tumble out of bed and head for my bathroom. But when I look in the mirror, I get another surprise.

This surprise is purple and glittery and it's all over my face!

I rub the sleepies out of my eyes and put my face up to the mirror for a closer look. Do I have chicken pox? No . . . I HAVE PURPLE GLITTER POX! I feel my head to see if I have a fever. And that's when I see the problem—my fingernails!

I polished them last night with the purple glitter polish Mary Ann gave me. Purple glitter polish is everywhere . . . except on my nails. I must have fallen asleep on my hands before my nails were dry. I can't go to school like this!

I race up the stairs to Mom's bathroom to get the polish remover. I pull bottles and jars out of her cabinet. I find the bottle I'm looking for—but it's empty!

What am I going to do?

I try rubbing my purple glitter pox off. I try scrubbing my purple glitter pox off. I even put my face in the bathroom sink and try soaking my purple glitter pox off.

Now my face is red and blotchy *and* purple and glittery.

I can just see my third-grade scrapbook. The first picture in it won't be pretty.

"Mallory, hurry up!" Mom calls from the kitchen. "You don't want to be late for your first day of school."

Actually, I do. I would love to be late. A whole year late.

I pull on capris and my best purple T-shirt. *What am I going to do?*

Then, I know. I know *exactly* what I'm going to do. I search through my closet until I find my ski mask. I pull it on and look in the mirror. Not bad. All you can see are my eyes, nose, and mouth. I will be the mystery girl of third grade.

"MALLORY!"

I pull my ski mask down a little further and head to the kitchen.

I sit down at the table and take a bite of pancakes. "Mmmm."

My brother Max looks at me like someone told a joke and he's the only one who didn't get it. "Why are you wearing a ski mask?"

"It's a new style." I take another bite. "A lot of third graders are doing it."

Max grabs my mask. "None that I know."

I try to keep my mask on, but Max is too fast. He stares at my face like he's just seen a two-headed zebra. "Mom! Dad! Look at Mallory!"

Mom drops her fork. Dad puts his newspaper down.

Now I know how the monkeys at the zoo must feel. Everyone is staring . . . AT ME! "We have to go to the drugstore before

school starts and buy some polish remover."

Mom shakes her head. "We don't have time to go to the store before school."

I pull my ski mask back on. "I can't go to school with purple dots on my face!"

Max yanks it off. "She can't go to school with a ski mask on either."

Mom inspects my face. "It's not that bad. You're going to school and the ski mask is staying home. That's final." She picks up her notebook. "School is waiting."

"Not so fast," says Dad. He pulls a camera out of a drawer. "Time for the McDonald family back-to-school picture."

Max groans. "Dad, not this year."

For once, I agree with Max.

Dad shakes his head, "It's tradition. Max, Mallory, over by the piano. Sherry, you too. After all, you're going back to school too."

Mom puts her arms around Max and me. "Smile," says Dad. He snaps our picture.

But as I follow Mom out the door, all I can think is that I don't have much to smile about. This day will go down as one of the worst ever. There will even be pictures to remind me of my horrible start to third grade.

Next door Joey and his dog, Murphy, are waiting for us in his front yard. Joey's sister, Winnie, and his dad, Mr. Winston, and his grandpa are there too.

"What happened to you?" Winnie looks at me like I'm contagious.

"You don't want to know," I mumble.

Joey studies my face like he's trying to figure out a tricky problem in math. "I have a ski mask if you want to borrow it."

Max laughs and tells Joey I don't need a ski mask.

Joey shrugs. "At least your face matches your shirt and your backpack. Everyone will know what your favorite color is as soon as they meet you."

Joey's dad smiles. "An excellent way of looking at things."

Mom starts down the sidewalk. "We're off to school!" she says. Winnie and Max follow Mom. Joey pats Murphy's head and falls in line. "We're off to school!"

I follow Joey. "We're off," I mumble.

But there's only one thing I'm off to . . . A BAD START!

HIDE-N-PEEK

There are lots of things I can't do with my head inside my backpack. Like find the way to my classroom. Even though Joey is guiding me through the maze of feet and stray notebooks, I have to work hard not to trip.

Joey stops. "There's a sign on the door." He reads out loud. "Mrs. Daily, Room 310. Welcome to Third Grade."

I can't believe I'm starting third grade in hiding. But I can just imagine what kids

22

would say if they could see my face.

"Check out the new kid."

"What's with the purple dots?"

"Where's she from? Jupiter?"

I don't want anybody to think I'm from another planet! My head's inside my backpack, and that's where it's staying.

"Good morning, class," says Mrs. Daily. "Please find the desk with your name tag on it and take a seat."

I move my backpack, just a little, so I can find the desk with the *Mallory McDonald* sticker. When I stick my name tag on my T-shirt, it goes on lopsided.

I sit down and peek at the girl in the chair next to me. She has on a rainbow T-shirt, matching glasses, and a perfectly straight name tag.

I wish Joey was in the chair next to me. But his desk is across the room next to another boy. I try to get his attention, but he doesn't see me. He's busy talking to the boy in the desk next to him.

Mrs. Daily taps a little green plastic frog on her desk. It croaks, and everyone stops talking. Mrs. Daily smiles and picks up the frog. "Class, this is Chester. When he opens his mouth, you will know it is time to close yours."

Great. Mary Ann's teacher keeps candy on her desk. Mine has a croaking frog.

Mrs. Daily keeps smiling. "The seat you are sitting in will be yours for the year. Let's all take a minute and introduce ourselves to our desk mates."

The girl in the rainbow T-shirt knocks on my backpack. "Anybody home?"

"Mallory McDonald. Like the restaurant, but no relation."

My desk mate leans over and peeks

inside my backpack. "Pamela Brooks. Why are you wearing a backpack on your head on the first day of school?"

I pull my head out of my backpack so Pamela can see my purple glitter pox.

She studies my face like she's a doctor and I'm getting a checkup. "You look better without the backpack."

I hope Pamela is right. I slide my backpack under my desk.

"OK, class," says Mrs. Daily. "Now that we know our desk mates, let's get to know each other. When it's your turn, please say your name and share something about yourself with the class. Who would like to start?"

Pamela raises her hand.

Mrs. Daily checks her seating chart. "Thank you for volunteering, Pamela."

Pamela stands up. "Hi everybody, my name is Pamela Brooks. I want to be a famous journalist when I grow up."

"You're in the right classroom." Mrs. Daily smiles. "We'll be doing a lot of writing this year. Our class is in charge of the school newspaper."

Mrs. Daily checks her seating chart. "Mallory, you're next."

I stand up. "My name is Mallory McDonald."

"She likes purple," says a voice.

There's giggling all around me.

I feel like I need to say why my face is purple. The problem is I don't want to say why it's *really* purple. Mary Ann would say this calls for some creative sharing.

I clear my throat. "This morning, I was polishing my cat's toenails when she started jumping all over the place."

I move my arms around to show what a wild, jumping cat looks like. "When I tried to calm her down, I got polish all over my face."

I turn around in a circle so everyone can see my purple dots. "I didn't want to be late on the first day of school, so I had to leave it on."

There's more giggling.

Mrs. Daily taps Chester's head. "Class, that's enough. Mallory moved here this summer and brought someone special to school with her. Mallory, why don't you tell the class who in your family is part of Fern Falls Elementary now."

"My mother is the new music teacher," I mumble.

"Mrs. McDonald has some wonderful plans for music this year," says Mrs. Daily. "You'll hear more when you meet Mrs. McDonald later this week."

Everybody stares at me. I wonder if this is how it's going to be all year . . . *Mallory McDonald, daughter of the music teacher.*

I try to pay attention while Mrs. Daily continues with the introductions.

Zack likes tomato sandwiches. Adam went to school in South Africa for a year. Sammy hates being the oldest because he gets blamed for everything. Emma collects rubber bands, glow rocks, and used paper. Grace collects shoes.

I try to remember who likes tomato sandwiches and who collects used paper, but my mind keeps thinking about my face and my mom.

Mrs. Daily calls on two girls who are desk mates.

Danielle and Arielle are Virgos and best friends.

They're lucky. They're best friends, *and* they're desk mates. I wonder who Mary Ann's desk mate is this year. I wonder if they'll become best friends.

Mrs. Daily calls on Joey. "I like skateboarding and soccer," says Joey.

His desk mate is Pete. "I like skateboarding and soccer too," says Pete. When Pete sits down, he and Joey high-five each other.

It looks like Joey likes his desk mate.

Nicholas, Brittany, Evan, April, Dawn, and Jackson introduce themselves. There are lots of names to remember.

Mrs. Daily spends the rest of the morning telling us about some of the units we'll be studying this year. Bears. Pilgrims. The United States of America.

When the lunch bell rings, we line up and follow Mrs. Daily to the cafeteria.

Someone behind me groans. I think it's a *we're-too-old-to-have-to-line-up-behind-the-teacher-and-walk-to the-cafeteria* groan. But I'm glad we do. I have no idea where the cafeteria is at this school. In my old school, I knew where everything was. I knew what to do. I even knew who to sit with at lunch. At this school, I have no idea.

When I get inside the cafeteria, I sit down next to Joey.

"Boys' table." He shrugs his shoulders. "Sorry."

I can't believe Joey doesn't want to eat lunch with me. Friends are supposed to eat lunch with friends. I always ate lunch with Mary Ann.

I pick up my lunch bag and go sit at the table with the girls from my class. But I feel like I should call it the *I-don't-have-anybody-to-talk-to-because-everybody-is-already-talking-to-somebody-else* table.

I unwrap my sandwich and take a bite. But when I do, I taste something awful . . . tuna fish! Max always gets tuna fish, and I always get peanut butter and marshmallow. Mom gave me the wrong sandwich on the first day of school!

I take another bite of tuna fish and gag.

I'm not sure if it's the tuna fish or every single thing about this day, but I'm starting to feel sick.

After lunch, Mrs. Daily gives us our first spelling list: *elbow, groans, shadows, bulldozer, coast, loan, cobra, over.*

I wish a bulldozer would run over me.

Two hours and forty-nine minutes until I'll be through with this day.

"Class," Mrs. Daily says. "We have a lot to look forward to this week. Tuesdays will be art days. So tomorrow, you'll have your first art class. On Wednesdays, you'll have P.E. And on Thursdays, music. This Thursday, you'll meet Mrs. McDonald."

When Mrs. Daily says "This Thursday, you'll meet Mrs. McDonald," everyone turns around and looks at me.

I groan. I wish I could run. I wish I could hide. I wish I could be anywhere but here right now . . . even Jupiter.

SINGING THE BLUES

I'm on a mission . . . a *Thursday-morning-make-a-wish-before-school* mission.

I live on a street called Wish Pond Road. There's a real wish pond on my street. I can throw stones into it and make all the wishes I want.

When I moved to Wish Pond Road, Joey told me that the shiny black stones are wish pebbles. He said if you find one, your wish will come true.

The only problem is that wish pebbles are hard to find.

I pick up a plain, white rock and throw it into the water. *I wish everybody will like my mom when they meet her today.*

I watch the pond water ripple where I threw in the stone.

I think back to Tuesday when we had art with Mrs. Pearl.

"We're going to have so much fun in art this year," she said. She told us that as third graders, we'd be studying lots of different kinds of art. Then she wrote the word *expressionism* on the board and explained what it meant.

"Expressionism is a type of art where the artist paints what he's feeling inside, not necessarily what things really look like in the outside world."

Mrs. Pearl held up a picture of some flowers. "This is a painting called 'Sunflowers' by a famous expressionist artist named Vincent Van Gogh."

Mrs. Pearl passed out paper and showed us how to sketch flowers. She said we'd be talking a lot about expressing ourselves through our artwork.

"Isn't Mrs. Pearl nice?" Pamela said as we walked back to Room 310.

I throw another rock into the water. Pamela was right. Mrs. Pearl is nice.

On Wednesday, we had P.E. with Coach Kelly.

When we got to the field, Coach Kelly blew his whistle. "No time like the present to get in shape." We lined up and did stretches and jumping jacks.

"You look like a bunch of professional athletes," said Coach Kelly.

Then he told us we were in training to run the mile. We ran laps around the track. He high-fived everybody as we passed him.

"Isn't Coach Kelly cool?" Joey whispered to me.

I throw another rock in the wish pond. *Everybody* likes Mrs. Pearl and Coach Kelly. I hope when everybody meets my mom today, they feel the same way about her.

"MALLORY!" Mom calls my name from down the street.

As I walk home, I think about what Mom said last night. She promised me she would do her best to be my mom at home and my music teacher at school. But Max told me I shouldn't count on that promise.

"Mallory, Mom is the music teacher. You're going to have to face the music." He laughed like crazy. "Get the joke?"

I got it. Even though Max said he

doesn't see what the big deal is about Mom teaching at our school, to me IT IS A VERY BIG DEAL!

So today I'm doing everything I can to make sure there's nothing to laugh about when the Fern Falls Elementary third graders meet my mom.

I made wishes at the wish pond. I'm wearing my four-leaf clover charm bracelet. I have on my lucky leopard socks, even though they're making the walk to school a hot and itchy one.

"Earth to Mallory," says Joey as we follow my mom to school.

"Huh?" I bend down to scratch my ankle.

"We're halfway to school," says Joey. "And you haven't said a word."

I slow down so Mom can't hear what I'm about to say. "I'm a little worried about everyone meeting my mom."

"How bad can it be?" asks Joey.

But that's just it. I don't know how bad it can be. I tried to talk to Mom last night about being nice like Mrs. Pearl or cool like Coach Kelly, but I don't think she was listening.

I think about Van Gogh. I wonder if he ever tried to express himself and nobody listened. I wonder if his mother was a teacher at his school.

As we walk into our classroom, Mrs. Daily tells everyone to take a seat. "We have a busy day," she says.

First, we say the Pledge of Allegiance. Then Mrs. Daily passes out our vocabulary worksheets. "If you don't know what any of the words mean, you can look them up in the dictionary in the back of the room."

One of our words is *nervous*.

I don't need a dictionary to know what *nervous* means.

"Class," says Mrs. Daily, when we're done with our worksheets. "I'm going to walk you down to the music room now. You're going to meet Mrs. McDonald. Please show her how well behaved Fern Falls Elementary third graders are. Does anybody have any questions before we go?"

I do. Can we learn long division instead?

"I can't wait to meet your mom," Pamela whispers in my ear.

When we walk into the music room, Mom tells everyone to take a seat. "Good morning, class." Mom smiles. "Welcome to music. I'm Mrs. McDonald."

But when Mom says *Mrs. McDonald,* everyone turns around and looks at me. I wish I could hide my head inside a songbook.

"We're going to have a lot of fun in music this year," Mom says. "We'll be putting on a special show at the end of October called Fall Festival."

Mom pauses. I think she's waiting for everyone to clap or cheer.

They might have clapped if she'd said:

We're going to have a lot of fun in music this year. We'll be going to a special concert for kids. It will be an all-day field trip with pizza and ice cream. But that's not what she said.

I think about how things used to be before we moved to Fern Falls. Mom gave piano lessons at home. Even though I had to walk around with cotton balls in my ears, I wish things were like they used to be.

"We're going to start the year off singing 'America,'" says Mom. "I want you to really think about what you're singing." Then she says the words really slowly like she's talking to a room full of two-year-olds.

My coun-try 'tis of thee,
Sweet land of li-ber-ty;
Of thee I sing.

Land where my fa-thers died
Land of the pil-grims' pride
From e-ver-y moun-tain side
Let free-dom ring.

She asks everybody to focus on the song
and repeat the words with her.

I try to focus on *My Country 'Tis of Thee*.
But the words *My Mom Embarrasses Me* just
keep popping into my head.

STREET FRIENDS

"Pass the Fruity Pops," says Mom.

Max and I look at each other. Mom never eats Fruity Pops.

Dad slides the box across the breakfast table. "You've only been at school for a week, and you're already eating like a kid," he says.

Mom laughs.

But I don't. Mom might be eating like a kid, but she's definitely not acting like one. This week at school, she did lots of things kids would NEVER do.

In the girls' bathroom, she reminded everybody to wash their hands. And in the cafeteria, she told the girls to be sure and eat their *healthies* first.

Kids NEVER do either of those things! It's no fun to be the kid whose mother reminds other kids to do that kind of stuff.

"I have good news," says Mom. "We're having dinner at the Winston's tonight."

That is good news, and I know someone else who will think so too. "Lucky Max." I make a kissy face. "He gets to see Winnie."

Max tries to hit me on the head with a cereal box, but the phone rings, and I grab it before Max can get to me.

"Hey! Hey! Hey!" says a voice on the other end.

It's Mary Ann!

"Hey! Hey! Hey!" I sit on top of the desk

and cross my legs. This is a great way to start my Saturday.

"How's school?" I ask Mary Ann.

Mary Ann tells me about Mrs. Thompson and her candy jar. She says third grade is awesome. She says school is the same as last year, only better.

"How's school for you?" Mary Ann asks.

Nothing is the same for me. Different school. Different friends. Different teachers, and Mom is one of them.

I tell Mary Ann about Fern Falls Elementary and Pamela and Mrs. Daily. Then I cover the phone with my hand. "Guess what? Mom is the music teacher at my school," I say in a soft voice.

Mary Ann giggles into the phone. "What's it like having your mom as a teacher?"

"I can't really talk now," I whisper into the phone. "But so far, not so good."

"Gotcha," says Mary Ann. "I can't really talk now either. Emily, Ellen, and Becca are coming over. We have to make a reptile collage for school."

I feel like my Fruity Pops are doing forward rolls in my stomach. If I still lived there, I'd be making a reptile collage at Mary Ann's house too. But the only kind of collage I can make is a "No Friends" collage.

"Have fun." I try to sound cheery as I tell Mary Ann good-bye. But when I hang up the phone, I make an *I-don't-feel-cheery* face.

Dad walks over to the desk. "Mallory, What's the matter? It's a beautiful Saturday morning, and you don't seem your usual sunny self."

"I'm not my usual self," I say. "My usual self would be at Mary Ann's house working on a project with all my friends. But I'm stuck here with no friends."

"Why don't you call Joey?" says Dad. "He's your friend."

"Joey has soccer practice."

"How about one of the other kids in your class," Mom says. "What about your desk mate, Pamela? Why don't you call her and see if she wants to come over."

I shake my head. "I hardly know Pamela."

Mom sits down in front of me. "If you call her, you'll get to know her."

I groan. Mom can be so predictable. I should have known she'd say something like that.

"Why don't we spend the day together?" I say to Mom. "We can do mother-daughter things, like paint our nails and go out for lunch."

Mom smiles. "I would love to, but I have lesson plans to do and I have to work on Fall Festival. It's right around the corner."

Mom pats my head. "You understand, don't you?"

I understand. I understand that now that Mom has two hundred students, she doesn't have time for her own two kids.

I go into my room and close the door. "Cheeseburger, it's just you and me today." I rub the fur behind her ears.

I think about what Dad said, about not being my sunny self. I pick up Cheeseburger and stand in front of the mirror in my bathroom. "Cheeseburger," I say out loud. "I proclaim today 'Let's Try Our Hardest to be Sunny' day."

We sit on the bed, and I paint my toenails. Then I get out the scrapbooks Mary Ann and I made. We always worked on our scrapbooks on the weekends.

I think about Joey.

I can't see him doing scrapbooks. He's too busy playing soccer and skateboarding. Even though we like to do some things together, we don't like doing *everything* together, the way Mary Ann and I did.

I flip through the pages of the second-grade scrapbook Mary Ann and I made. "A lot has changed since last year, hasn't

it?" I say to Cheeseburger. But when I look at her, her eyes are closed. I think trying to be sunny made her sleepy.

After lunch, I read and watch TV until Mom says it's time to get ready to go over to the Winston's house.

When we get to their house, Joey opens the door before we even ring the doorbell.

"What took you so long?" he asks. "I've

got something to show you." Max and I
follow Joey into the kitchen. Winnie is at
the kitchen table surrounded by piles of
playing cards. She's feeding them into a
little machine.

"What's that?" I ask.

Winnie rolls her eyes like she's not
surprised that I don't know what it is.

"It's an automatic card shuffler," says

Joey. "You put the cards in, and the machine does all the shuffling. Dad ordered it for us off the Internet."

"Cool," says Max.

"Very cool," says Joey. "Do you guys want to play Crazy Eights?"

"I don't know how," I tell him. "But I can

play Go Fish. Can we play that instead?"

Joey nods. "It's not my favorite, but we can play it if you want."

Winnie rolls her eyes again, but she and Joey and Max and I play Go Fish until Mr. Winston says it's time for dinner.

We eat pizza and make our own sundaes.

During dessert, Joey's grandpa asks about school. "So is the school year off to a good start for you youngsters?" he asks.

"It's OK." Joey shrugs his shoulders. "I like summer better."

"It's great!" Winnie smiles at her grandfather. "Now that we're in fifth grade, Max and I get our own lockers and we get to change classes. Max is in my math class. Don't you think Mrs. Mansberg is the world's *best* math teacher?" Winnie asks Max.

Max swallows a spoonful of strawberry ice cream and nods his head. "The best," he says.

Someone must have squirted whipped cream in my ears. I'm definitely hearing things. All Max ever says is that Mrs. Mansberg is the *worst* teacher in the school. I think Winnie could say fried eggs taste good on ice cream and Max would agree with her.

After dessert, we say good night and go home. Mom tells Max and me to brush our teeth and get ready for bed.

I put on my panda bear pajamas and go into the bathroom to brush my teeth. Max is already at the sink.

I squeeze some toothpaste onto my toothbrush. "World's *best* night, huh?"

Max spits. "I guess so."

I guess so. "I can't believe you didn't

think it was super. Winnie was sooooo friendly." I bat my eyes. "Maybe she likes you as much as you like Mrs. Mansberg."

Max wipes his mouth with a towel. "For your information, she does like me . . . on the street and when no one else is around. At school, she acts like she doesn't even

know I'm in her math class."

He tosses the towel in the hamper. "That's what you call a *street friend.*"

I turn off the tap. "I've never heard of a street friend."

"Learn something new every day."

I think about Joey.

He sits at the boys' table in the cafeteria. He goes to soccer practice on the weekends. On Thursday, when Mrs. Daily had us pick partners for a science project, Joey picked Pete.

The only time he really plays with me is when we're together on our street. And when we're on our street, he's really nice. Like tonight, he even played the card game I wanted to play.

"You don't think Joey is my street friend, do you?"

Max shrugs. "Like sister, like brother,

if you ask me."

If you ask me, making new friends isn't easy. I hope Max is wrong about Joey. I go into my room and get into bed. I can't sleep, so I try counting sheep. But I end up counting friends instead.

And the trouble is . . . I don't get very far.

STARS EVERYWHERE

"Class, take your seats please," says Mom. "I have some exciting news."

I groan. One of the cool parts about having your mom as a teacher is you know what she's going to say before everybody else does. One of the not-so-cool parts is that you know when she's going to say something that nobody will think is cool.

Today is one of those days.

"As many of you know," Mom says. "The third grade at Fern Falls Elementary always puts on Fall Festival. This year's show is *Down on the Farm*."

I hear giggles from the back of the classroom. Someone whispers, "Mrs. McDonald had a farm."

I knew it! This show is *way* too babyish. At dinner last night, I tried to tell Mom that *Down on the Farm* is too babyish for third graders. Max laughed and said third graders *are* babyish.

Mom said it would be a great show.

She waits for the giggling to stop before she continues. "Fall Festival will be bigger and better than ever. We're going to put together committees to work on costumes, sets, lighting, and makeup."

Pete raises his hand. "When is the show?"

"At the end of October," says Mom. "So we have a lot to do to get ready."

Danielle and Arielle raise their hands. "Can we be in charge of makeup?"

"I'll keep you two in mind," Mom says.

Pamela raises her hand. "I think Fall Festival will be a lot of fun. I can't wait to work on sets and costumes."

Mom smiles at Pamela. "I'm glad you're excited."

All teachers, including my own mother, spend a lot of time smiling at Pamela.

Mom takes a cowboy hat out of the closet and says, *"Down on the Farm* is the story of Farmer Brown and his wife. They grow fruits and vegetables on their farm. Farmer Brown tries selling his fruits and vegetables to the townspeople, but no one wants to buy them. They would rather eat pizza and hamburgers."

Mom continues. "Farmer Brown is upset. He doesn't know what to do. Mrs. Brown comes up with a plan.

"She invites everyone in the town to a giant feast made from the fruits and vegetables they grow on the farm. The food tastes so delicious, the townspeople start buying everything, and Farmer Brown is happy."

Mom holds the cowboy hat in the air.

"Now, we're going to draw to see who will have which roles. Line up," Mom says. "And remember, this is about working together to make a great show. All of the roles are important."

Even though I think this show is kind of stupid, I hope I get a good role.

Joey picks first. He waves a little piece of paper in the air. "I'm Farmer Brown!"

I never thought of Joey as an actor, but he looks happy about his role.

Arielle and Danielle pick next. They both get to be rain fairies. I don't know how they always get to do everything together.

Everyone draws slips of paper out of the hat. There are lots of good parts: farmhands and townspeople. There are lots of not-so-good parts too: fruits and vegetables.

When it's my turn to pick, I cross my toes and make a wish. *Please let me be Mrs. Brown.* I stick my hand in the hat and pull out a piece of crumpled-up paper. I uncrumple it. I'm not Mrs. Brown. I'm an . . . *eggplant.*

I don't want to be an eggplant! I would rather be an apple or a potato. An eggplant has to be the worst role in the show.

Pamela picks next. "Mrs. Brown," she yells. "I get to be Farmer Brown's wife!"

It's not fair! Pamela is Mrs. Brown and I'm an eggplant! I sit down, unroll the sliver of paper in my hand, and read it again.

Brittany looks over my shoulder. "You're an eggplant. I'm a bowl of cherries."

"It's the pits, isn't it?"

Brittany doesn't laugh. "It's going to be

really fun. Making our costumes and all
that other stuff your mom said. Who cares
what role you have?"

I do. I take my paper over to Mom
and tap her on the shoulder. "Uh, Mom, I
mean, Mrs. McDonald." I'm not even sure
what to call my own mom. "I need to

redraw," I whisper in her ear. "I don't want
to be an eggplant."

"You'll make a fine eggplant," Mom
whispers in my ear. She tells me to sit
down. Then she asks everyone to take
their seats.

I can't believe it. My own mom won't

let me redraw. I'm her daughter, and she's treating me like I'm just another kid. This is so unfair!

Pamela passes a note folded into a neat square to me. I open it up.

Mallory, I'm so excited!!! I can't believe I get to be the farmer's wife.

Are you:

A. So excited about your part?

B. Going to work on the costume committee?

C. Feeling like this is going to be the best Fall Festival ever?

I'm all three!!! Pamela

I consider Pamela's note for about two seconds. I know Pamela is A, B, and C.

But I'm D . . . none of the above. I DON'T WANT ANY PART OF THIS SHOW.

I shove Pamela's note in my pocket. I think about what Mom said, about giving Pamela a chance. I'm trying, but that's hard to do when she does things that annoy me, like writing this silly note.

Mary Ann and I used to pass notes, but that was different because she used to pass notes I liked reading.

When the bell rings, Mom waves as we leave her classroom. "We'll start learning the songs for the show next week," she says. "And remember, you're all stars."

But I don't feel like a star. I feel like an eggplant.

On the way home from school, Joey can't stop talking about Fall Festival. "It will be so great," he says. "We can practice our parts together."

"I won't need to practice," I tell Joey. "All an eggplant does is lay in a bowl."

Joey shrugs. "You don't know what you'll have to do yet."

I don't know what I'll have to do, but I'm pretty sure I won't want to do it.

At dinner, I tell Mom I don't want to be an eggplant. "Don't you think as the daughter of the music teacher, I should get to be the farmer's wife or a rain fairy?"

Mom puts a piece of chicken on my plate. "Mallory, we drew out of a hat."

"It's the perfect role for you," says Max. "You kind of look like an eggplant."

I try to ignore Max. I watch Mom spoon mashed potatoes onto my plate. "Fall Festival will be fun," she says. "It's about working together with your classmates. I'm sure you'll enjoy it."

I shake my head.

Mom puts her arm around me. "You'll make a very cute eggplant," she says. "Why don't you write Mary Ann and invite her to come see you in Fall Festival?"

The last thing I want is for Mary Ann to see me dressed up like an eggplant. I cross my arms.

"C'mon, Sweet Potato," says Dad. "Where's that good old Mallory spirit?"

It used to be just Mom who called me Sweet Potato, but now Dad does it too.

I look inside my milk glass and underneath my placemat. "I can't find it anywhere!" I tell Dad. "So you might as well change my name from *Sweet* Potato to *Unhappy* Eggplant."

THE DAILY NEWS

"Calling all columnists." Mrs. Daily taps Chester on the head. "Would anyone here like to be in the newspaper business?"

Hands shoot up everywhere.

"Class, we're going to publish a newspaper for the whole school to read," says Mrs. Daily. "We'll publish one issue per month. Does anyone know the main function of a newspaper?"

Pamela's hand is up high. Mrs. Daily points to her.

"To give information to people," Pamela says.

"Excellent, Pamela." Mrs. Daily writes the word *information* on the chalkboard. "What kind of information do you think we should include in our newspaper?"

"Sports scores," Pete shouts.

"Horoscopes," Danielle and Arielle say together.

"Comics," says Zack.

"News," suggests Adam.

"Advice," says Emma.

Mrs. Daily writes *sports scores, horoscopes, comics, news,* and *advice* on the chalkboard. "I think we should include all of this information in our paper," she says.

Then she writes something else on the board—*Profile: A description of someone's abilities, personality, or career.*

"Class, we're going to learn how to write

profiles. We'll be picking one teacher at Fern Falls Elementary to write about for each issue of our paper. We'll call that our Teacher-of-the-Month column."

I raise my hand. "Mrs. Daily, how will we decide which teachers to write about?"

"Good question, Mallory. We'll pick Fern Falls Elementary teachers who are doing special things that other students might find interesting."

Pamela leans over to my side of the desk. "I'm going to tell Mrs. Daily we should pick her for the first issue. Students will find it interesting that we're writing a newspaper."

I'm not sure other students will think that's interesting, but I'm sure Mrs. Daily will like the idea. It bugs me that Pamela always says things Mrs. Daily likes hearing.

I rub my forehead with my pinkies.

Mary Ann and I used to do that when we were trying to think of something good to say.

Right now, I want to think of something to say that Mrs. Daily will like hearing.

"Now," says Mrs. Daily. "We need to pick a name for our paper. Any ideas?"

Everyone starts whispering. I keep rubbing.

Then I remember something Mom said.

"Maybe we should call it *The Daily News*," I whisper to Pamela. "Get it? Mrs. Daily. *Daily News*. Do you think Mrs. Daily will like that?"

Pamela's hand flies up in the air. "How about *The Daily News*?" she blurts out. She doesn't even wait for Mrs. Daily to call on her.

"Hmmm." Mrs. Daily rubs her chin. "It's catchy. Let's see a show of hands.

Who likes the name *The Daily News* for our newspaper?"

Hands shoot up everywhere.

"It's settled then." Mrs. Daily writes *The Daily News* in big, bold letters on the chalkboard. "Our newspaper will be called *The Daily News*. Let's all thank Pamela for the wonderful suggestion."

Everyone claps. Everyone but me.

PAMELA STOLE MY IDEA! I thought of something Mrs. Daily would like hearing and Pamela took the words right out of my mouth.

Everyone is busy talking about *The Daily News*. But not me. I'm busy trying to figure out what I want to say to Pamela.

And the answer is not much. I don't care if I ever speak to Pamela again.

"Settle down." Mrs. Daily taps Chester. "Everyone in this class will be part of the paper. I want each of you to give some thought to what you'd like to write."

What I'd like to write is a want ad:

WaNted.
New desk mate. Kind and friendly. THieves don't apply. ConTacT MaLLoRy McPoNaLd. FeRN FaLLS ELemeNtaRy. RooM 310. Row 2. Seat 6.

I tried giving Pamela a chance, but if you ask me, it was a flop. I can't believe she stole my idea. I always told Mary Ann my good ideas, and she never took them. I don't know if desk mates can officially not speak to each other, but I'm officially not speaking to Pamela.

"Now," says Mrs. Daily. "Unless someone can think of something else we should include in our newspaper, let's open our math books."

Joey raises his hand. "I can think of something else we should include. How about announcements?"

Mrs. Daily smiles. "What kind of announcements did you have in mind?"

"You know, stuff that's going on in school, like the date of the Fall Festival."

"Joey, that's a wonderful idea. *The Daily News* announcement column. I like it."

I don't! I don't want to announce Fall Festival to the whole school. Maybe Joey wants everyone to see him—he's Farmer Brown. But I don't want anyone to see me!

Mrs. Daily taps Chester on the head, and the classroom gets quiet.

"The newspaper will be lots of fun.

We'll start working on it next week. Class, please open your math textbooks to page sixty-two."

I open mine to page sixty-two. Word problems. Long, complicated word problems fill the page from top to bottom.

I sigh. Page sixty-two and I have a lot in common.

We're both full of problems.

LETTER
WRITING

I'm being held prisoner . . . by my mother! She says I have a lot of writing to do, and I can't go outside until I do it.

I have to write my article for *The Daily News,* and I have to write to Mary Ann and invite her to Fall Festival. I know why I have to write the article for *The Daily News.* It's due Monday. But I don't know why I have to write to Mary Ann.

Mom says there's nothing more exciting than getting an invitation in the mail. I told her I can think of a lot of things that are more exciting.

But Mom said she's been asking me to write this letter for over two weeks, and I'm stuck in my room until the letter and the article are written.

I pull out a sheet of paper. I'm going to write my article first.

On Friday, Pamela told me she'd be working on what she's writing for the newspaper *all* weekend. "Doesn't that sound like fun?" she asked me.

"Fun, fun, fun," I mumbled. But being stuck in my room writing doesn't sound like fun, fun, fun to me. I pick up Cheeseburger and put her on top of my desk.

Cheeseburger purrs and closes her eyes. But I open mine. Cheeseburger just gave me a great idea! I start writing. My article doesn't take long at all.

When I finish, I take out another sheet of paper so I can start on my letter. But getting started isn't easy.

I want to see Mary Ann, but I don't want Mary Ann to see me dressed up as

an eggplant. I rub my forehead for a long
time, and then I begin.

Dear Mary Ann,

Do you remember I told you that my
mom is the new music teacher at my
school? Well, she is making the third
graders do a show called Fall Festival.

It is about a farmer and the vegetables
on his farm. I am an eggplant in the show.
It is a silly and babyish show!

Mom told me to write you a letter and
invite you and your mom to come and see
the show. YOU DEFINITELY DO NOT HAVE
TO COME.

I want you to come and visit, but
another time will be MUCH better.

If you have to sit through the show, you
will be bored. Bored. Bored. Bored. So it

is probably best if you don't come for Fall Festival.

After you read this letter, rip it up and forget I even sent it. OK?

That's it.

I hope you're eating lots of candy out of Mrs. Thompson's jar. If I were in her class, that's what I would be doing.

G.2.G. (Got to go!)

Hugs and Kisses, Mallory

I reread my letter. I really don't want Mary Ann to come to Fall Festival.

I think back to the last practice. I didn't even do anything until the end of the show when I sang a song with a bunch of other vegetables.

I don't know what the big deal is about seeing me do that.

I reread my letter. Then I lick the envelope shut and seal it with a kiss . . . an *I-sure-hope-this-works-and-Mary-Ann-won't-come-to-Fall-Festival* kiss.

TEACHER-OF-THE-MONTH

"IT'S OUT!" screams Pamela.

"What's out?" I check the floor around my desk. "A rat? A mouse? A snake?"

"No, silly." Pamela shoves the first issue of *The Daily News* in my face and starts jumping up and down like a cheerleader in the last minute of a tied game. "It's soooo exciting!" she squeals.

I walk to the front of the classroom and

get a copy of *The Daily News* off of Mrs.
Daily's desk. I search through the Table of
Contents until I find what I'm looking for. I
flip to page seven, cross my toes, and read.

HOW TO GET YOUR CAT TO NAP
by Mallory McDonald
(Dedicated to Cheeseburger, my cat, who is
a great napper)

Most cats love to nap. But if you
have the kind of cat that prefers to
be awake, here are some tips to get
your cat to sleep.
   Tip #1: Sing your cat a lullaby.
(Don't try this if you sing off-key.
Your cat might get mad and stay
awake forever.)
   Tip #2: Draw a picture for your

cat of other cats sleeping. (Once she sees that cats are doing this everywhere, she might want to try it herself.)

Tip #3: Make your cat watch while you do your homework. (I promise this will put your cat to sleep!)

Tip #4: If your cat is already sleeping (this is my best advice), DON'T WAKE HER UP!

If you need help with any of these tips, ask Mallory McDonald, local cat expert.

My article isn't bad. In fact, it's pretty good. Cats should be sleeping all over Fern Falls by the end of the day.

But I don't get a chance to admire it for long before Pamela starts squealing again. "Mal-lor-y, did you see my Teacher-of-the-Month column on page three?"

She looks over my shoulder and waits for me to read it.

Even though I'm officially not speaking to Pamela, I flip to page three and start reading.

TEACHER-OF-THE-MONTH:
Fern Falls Elementary Third Grade
Teacher, Mrs. Daily
by Pamela Brooks (her devoted student)

Mrs. Daily is the third grade teacher at Fern Falls Elementary.

Mrs. Daily makes learning fun! She makes learning science fun! She makes learning social studies fun! She makes learning math fun!

Mrs. Daily makes learning so much fun that even when you're learning, you feel like you're at recess!

Mrs. Daily is SUPER! It was her idea to publish this SUPER newspaper!

I asked Mrs. Daily if she could tell us the secret to her success as a teacher.

"You have to love what you do to do a good job at it, and I love what I do," says Mrs. Daily.

I love what she does too and so do a lot of third graders at Fern Falls Elementary.

So let's all give a big cheer for Mrs. Daily.

Hip, hip, hooray! Hip, hip, hooray! Hip, hip, hooray!

Thank you, Mrs. Daily, for being the best teacher ever!!!!!!!!!!!!!!

I close my newspaper. I've read enough.

Pamela tugs on my sleeve. "Mrs. Daily said she looooved my article, and the apple I gave her for being Teacher-of-the-Month."

I roll my newspaper into a cone, in case I have to barf. I'm sure Mrs. Daily looooved Pamela's article and her apple. She loooooves everything Pamela does. But I don't! I reopen my newspaper and pretend to read the school lunch menus.

Mrs. Daily taps Chester on the head. "Class, you should be proud of the first issue of *The Daily News.* You all worked hard. Does anybody have any comments?"

Joey raises his hand. "Did everybody see my announcement column?"

I unroll my paper. Joey's announcement column is on page four. Dress rehearsal for Fall Festival is next Thursday night.

My last eggplant-free weekend.

I think about all the times we've practiced our songs in music class. It's one thing to sing like an eggplant but another thing to dress like one.

Pamela leans over my shoulder and reads the announcement column. "Dress rehearsal is next week. It's soooo exciting," she squeals. "Even though we've been practicing in class, won't it be exciting when we finally get to rehearse on the stage?"

I put my head on my desk and groan.

I'm trying to get excited. But some things are hard to get excited about.

Having Pamela Brooks as a desk mate is one of those things.

Being an eggplant in Fall Festival is another.

DRESS REHEARSAL

"Eat your meatball," says Mom.

I push my plate away.

I don't want to eat my meatball. I also don't want to put on my eggplant costume and go to the auditorium tonight for dress rehearsal, and that's what I have to do as soon as I finish eating my meatball.

"C'mon," says Mom. "I can't be late."

I take a teeny tiny bite of meatball and spit it in my napkin. "This tastes funny."

"Mallory!" Mom says my name like I'm going to ruin the whole night if I don't eat what's on my plate.

Dad sticks his fork in the meatball on his plate and takes a bite. "New recipe?"

Mom puts a bowl of spaghetti on the table. "Actually, they're frozen. I've been so busy with Fall Festival, I haven't had time to cook."

I look at Mom. She's wearing a T-shirt that says *Director* on it. It should say *All I care about is this stinkin' show.* Fall Festival is ALL she cares about these days.

Mom looks at me. "Mallory, hurry up."

I stick a fork into my meatball and hold it up to the light. "Who invented frozen meatballs?"

Mom groans.

I continue inspecting my meatball. "Maybe the astronauts did. They kind of

look like moon rocks."

Max shoves a big bite in his mouth. "Who cares who invented them?" Max helps himself to two more meatballs. "They're great. You'd know if you'd eat yours."

Easy for Max to say. He doesn't care if he has to eat a frozen meatball, just like he doesn't care that Mom is the music teacher at our school. But Max and I are different, because I do care.

I take a teeny, tiny bite. Then I give Mom an *I'm-going-to-be-sick* look.

Mom takes my plate and dumps it in the garbage. "We don't have time for this," she says.

She picks up the phone and calls the Winston's. She tells Joey to come over because it's time to go.

"Tonight will be awesome," says Joey when we're in the van. "I can't wait to rehearse on stage. It will be really different from doing it in the classroom."

Mom smiles at him in the rearview mirror. When we pull into the parking lot, Mom asks Joey and me to carry an armload of costumes.

Mom follows us into the auditorium.

"Careful, Mallory," she says. "Your costumes are dragging. You don't want anything to happen to them, do you?"

"Actually, I do," I whisper to Joey. "I want them to drop off a cliff."

I wait for Joey to laugh. But he doesn't. "Mallory, you should change your attitude. Fall Festival will be lots of fun."

Fun for him . . . he has a great part. He didn't have to invite his best friend to come watch him.

When we get inside the auditorium, Mom starts spreading the costumes out on chairs. The auditorium is filling up with Fern Falls Elementary third graders.

"OK, everyone." Mom looks at her clipboard. "Let's get into these costumes."

Joey puts on a straw hat. Pamela ties a red-checkered apron around her waist. The townspeople roll up the hems of their blue jeans and tuck in their white T-shirts.

Fruits and vegetables are putting on their costumes. Produce is popping up everywhere. There's a peach, a plum, an apple, and a bowl of cherries. There's a carrot, a radish, a string bean, and two lettuce leaves.

Mom asks me to adjust the stem on a

cluster of grapes. Then she helps me step into my eggplant costume. She starts pinning on my stem.

"Hold still," she says. "I don't want to stick you."

"What would happen if you did?" I ask. "Would eggplant juice drip out?" I laugh at my joke.

But Mom doesn't.

Joey looks at me like I'm a circus monkey who won't cooperate with the trainer. "Be serious," he says. "Fall Festival is tomorrow night, and we have a lot of work to do."

Did I hear him right? Did Joey tell me to be serious? If you ask me, Joey is taking Fall Festival *way* too seriously.

"OK, everyone," says Mom. "I want to take a quick picture before we get started. Fruits in front, vegetables in the back, townspeople and farmers squat in the middle. Everybody smile and say *salad*!"

I think about the picture. If I make a scrapbook of Fall Festival, it will look more like a cookbook than a scrapbook.

Mom blows her whistle. "Places everyone. Let's stick to the schedule." She sits in the front row of the auditorium while we sing all our songs.

First, the farmer sings. Then his wife sings. Then the townspeople sing. Then the fruits make a singing fruit salad.

When the vegetables go on stage, I waddle behind Dawn the string bean. The vegetables make a circle around the lettuce leaves and sing our song.

What would you do if no one ate the stew?
How would you feel if you got a raw deal?
Everyone should eat at least five a day.
Ask any vegetable, and that's what they'll say.

When we're done, the lettuce leaves sing the salad finale.

"Bravo!" Mom shouts when they finish. "Tomorrow night will be a smashing success."

When I get home, I'm going to the wish pond to wish that somehow, some way, this show will close before it ever opens.

But when I get home, Max hands me a letter. "It's from Mary Ann," he says.

I rip it open and start reading.

Dear Mallory,

Mom says we wouldn't miss the Fall Festival for anything. We think you will make a very cute eggplant!!! We're driving up Friday after school so we'll get there in time for the show. But Mom says we have to drive back Saturday morning.

SEE YOU SO, SO, SO SOON!

CAN'T WAIT, WAIT, WAIT!

FALL FESTIVAL WILL BE THE BEST!

Hugs and Kisses, Mary Ann

I rub my eyes. I can't believe Mary Ann is coming to Fall Festival.

I crumple up her letter and aim for the trash. Max catches it midair and reads it. "For once, Birdbrain is right. You'll make an adorable eggplant."

"Be serious," I tell Max. "As my big brother, you could try to help me think of something so I won't look stupid on stage."

"You're right." Max hands me Mary Ann's letter. He looks serious. "How about dancing lessons?" Max puffs out his cheeks and dances around the room like an overgrown eggplant. Then he falls on the floor laughing.

I crumple up Mary Ann's letter and throw it in the trash. "I hope you laugh so hard your head falls off," I tell Max.

I run to my room and slam my door. But even after I do, I can still hear Max laughing.

And the truth is, I don't blame him. I'm sure the sight of *Mallory the Dancing Eggplant* live on stage will be just hilarious.

A BROKEN LEG

Joey and I stop and read the sign on the bulletin board outside the auditorium:

"Fall Festival Tonight," he says out loud.

I can tell reading that sign makes Joey feel terrific. But it makes me feel sick. I feel my head. I think I have a fever . . . Fall Festival Fever.

I know if I tell Mom, she'll just say, "The show must go on!" Max says that's "show talk." Lately, that's the only kind of talk I hear from Mom.

Backstage, Mom zips kids into costumes. "Who's excited for Fall Festival?" she asks.

This must be a trick question. Who could possibly be excited?

But I look around and see lots of kids who look excited—Joey, Pamela, even Zack and Adam, who are lettuce leaves, look excited.

I pull my eggplant stem down on my head. I think I'm the only one around here who's NOT. I waddle over to a chair and sit down.

I think about this afternoon when Mary Ann and her mom got to our house.

As soon as they pulled into the driveway, Mary Ann popped out of the car and started hugging me like crazy.

"You're going to be a star!" She was jumping and dancing around me. She even tried to pick me up. "I know a stage star! I know a stage star!"

"Cut it out," I mumbled to Mary Ann.

But her mom heard me. "She's just excited to see you onstage tonight, and so am I." She rumpled my hair. "We wouldn't drive three hours to see anybody but you."

Then Mary Ann started jumping all over me again. "I want to see your costume!"

So I took Mary Ann to my room and showed her my costume.

"Try it on," she squealed.

I modeled my costume for Mary Ann. "I look ridiculous, don't I?" I was hoping Mary Ann would say, *"No, you look really, really, really cute."*

But that's not what she said. She didn't say anything . . . she couldn't, because she couldn't stop laughing!

I crossed my arms across my chest.

"Look." Mary Ann was trying to keep a

straight face. "It could be worse. You could have been an onion or a turnip. At least your costume is a good color."

But I could tell Mary Ann didn't think there was anything *good* about it.

Backstage, I wiggle in my chair and straighten my stem. Crowd noises are starting to fill the auditorium.

I pretend like I'm at the wish pond and make a wish: *I wish there was some way I could get out of this show.* But I don't think wishing will do much good.

Mom claps her hands. "Listen up, everybody. The show starts in just a few minutes, so find your places backstage."

I walk to my place near the front curtain and peek at the auditorium. It's filling up with people. I see Dad, Mary Ann, her mom.

As Mom says, *The show must go on.* But I can't wait until it's over.

"One minute till showtime," says Mom. "Quiet everyone."

Someone pulls the stem on top of my eggplant hat. I turn around. It's Max.

"What are you doing back here?" I whisper.

"I wanted to tell you to break a leg."

"Huh?" I can't believe my own brother wants me to break a leg!

"It's show talk." Max gives me a thumbs-up sign. "It means good luck on stage."

Max goes, but he leaves me with an idea . . . a thumbs-up idea. If I pretend like I broke my leg, I won't have to be *Mallory the Dancing Eggplant.*

That's it! All I have to do is find the right time to pretend like I broke it.

"Showtime," says Mom. "Concentrate and have fun."

I am concentrating . . . on breaking my leg. I've never broken a leg before. I've

never even pretended to break one.

Joey goes on stage first. He reads a page from Farmer Brown's journal about how much he loves his farm and his fruits and vegetables.

He sings a song, "No One Gives a Hoot about Veggies and Fruit."

When he's finished, the audience claps.

I squirm. I can't break my leg just standing here.

Then it's Pamela's turn. She reads a poem about wanting to save the farm. She sings "Let's Have a Feast." More clapping. Still no chance to break a leg.

When the townspeople go on stage, they sing "We Love Junk Food."

I watch a peach, a plum, an apple, some grapes, and a bowl of cherries go on stage. I listen as they sing the song they've practiced in music class.

Fruit, glorious fruit.
We hope you will try it.
Three pieces a day
Makes a healthy diet.
Just picture a great big peach—
Plump, juicy, and cute.
Oh fruit! Glorious fruit,
Glorious fruit, glorious fruit.

I wish I could find a glorious way to break my leg.

Emma the peach holds up a sign for the audience that says, *GO BANANAS!* There's clapping and whistling, just like Mom said there would be.

Still no chance for me to break a leg.

Mom motions for the vegetables to go on stage.

I follow a carrot, a potato, a radish, a string bean, and two lettuce leaves on stage. The vegetables make a circle around the lettuce leaves.

I walk to the back of the circle. Then I see it—the crate! Onstage, there's a little crate I'm supposed to stand on while we sing.

It's the chance I've been waiting for. All I have to do is pretend to trip when I'm stepping onto the crate, and I won't have to do my part in the show.

I walk toward the crate. Two more steps. I take a deep breath, close my eyes, and step up. I hope this works.

I pretend to trip and fall on the floor. "AAARGH! My leg! It's broken!"

It's not easy to clutch your leg and roll around in pain when you're wrapped up in five yards of purple felt, but I do.

Mom runs onto the stage. The vegetables turn around to see what's going on. Everybody in the auditorium is looking at me, and that's the one thing I didn't want anybody to be looking at!

Mom pokes my leg. "Can you move it?"

"Oooh!" I moan like people do on TV when they're really hurt and wiggle my ankle. "Just a little," I whisper.

Mom helps me stand up. "Let's go backstage and put ice on it. The show can continue." Mom motions the vegetables to start without me. Backstage, I sit in a chair. Mom inspects my leg. "Are you OK?"

"I think so." I adjust the ice pack and watch while everybody does the finale

we've been practicing in music class since the second week of school.

But Mom isn't watching the finale. She's watching me. "Don't you want to see the end of the show?" I ask her. She shakes her head.

Part of me is glad I'm not on stage singing, but part of me wishes I was. It would be better than sitting back here with Mom staring at me.

Clapping fills the auditorium. The show is over. Everyone comes backstage.

Pamela gives Mom flowers. "Thank you, Mrs. McDonald," she says. "This was the best Fall Festival ever."

Joey puts his fingers in his mouth, whistles, and yells "Yee-haw!" He sounds more like a cowboy than a farmer, but everybody laughs.

"I'm proud of all of you," says Mom.

"You did a wonderful job. There's a party in the auditorium. Punch and cookies for everyone."

Kids start running to the refreshment table. Everyone looks like they feel great.

Almost everyone. My leg is fine, but the rest of me feels awful. I thought I would feel good if I didn't have to be in the show, but now I wish Mom was saying she was proud of me too. I stay in my chair and hold the ice pack on my leg.

People start crowding around me. Dad, Joey, Pamela. Even though they ask if I'm OK, I feel like they all know what they're looking at . . . a leg that's not broken.

"Way to ruin a show," Max whispers in my ear. Winnie is standing behind him with her arms crossed. "My brother's chance at stardom washed down the drain."

I ignore Winnie and rearrange my ice

pack. "Max, you're the one who told me to break my leg!"

"Show talk, remember?" says Max.

Mary Ann brings me some punch and cookies. She hands me the plate, but I put it down. I love punch and cookies, but I'm not in the mood for a party.

When we get home, Mom takes out towels for Mary Ann and her mom.

"Maybe your family needs a few minutes alone," says Mary Ann's mom.

Mom nods her head like that's exactly what we need. "Mallory, you and Mary Ann get ready for bed, then Dad and I would like to see you in our room."

I pull on my flower power pajamas.

"I brought the same ones." Mary Ann pulls hers on too. She flips her head over and brushes her hair. "Too bad we didn't get to see you perform tonight."

I sit down on the floor, beside Mary Ann. I always know what I want to say to my best friend, but right now, I'm not so sure.

Mary Ann stops brushing. "I think your mom wants to talk about what happened tonight."

I want to talk about it too, and I do. I tell Mary Ann about all the things that have changed in my life since I started school in Fern Falls.

I tell her how hard it has been to start a new school.

I tell her that it hasn't been much fun taking Mom with me.

I tell her Mom doesn't have much time to be my mom, like she used to.

Mary Ann sits down on the bed beside me. "Remember when my parents got divorced? Everything changed. And then after a while, I got used to it."

I think about what Mary Ann said. "Do you think I'll ever get used to the way things are now?"

Mary Ann nods and smiles.

Max sticks his head in my room. "News flash: you're in big trouble! You better get upstairs on the double!"

Max is right. I slip my feet into my fuzzy duck slippers and trudge upstairs to Mom and Dad's room. I feel like I'm entering the

Chamber of Doom.

Mom tells me to sit on the bed. She crosses her arms. "Mallory, I know you weren't excited about the show. Did you fall on purpose?"

When I swallow, I feel like I've got a cement truck stuck in my throat.

I wish I could be anywhere but here right now . . . in a junkyard, a sewer plant, even

a swamp filled with quicksand and hungry alligators.

I nod. It's a tiny nod, but it's big enough for Mom to know the truth.

She shakes her head. "Mallory, what you did was wrong. You let your classmates down. You let the audience down. You let me down."

Mom keeps talking. "Sometimes we all have to do things we don't want to do, and that's what you should have done. Sometimes we have to consider other people's feelings, not just our own."

My feet feel cold, even inside my fuzzy duck slippers.

Mom is quiet for a minute, but her face is all pinched up, like a raisin. "Mallory, is there something you'd like to say?"

Actually, there are a lot of things I'd like to say. I think about the expressionist paintings we're working on in art class. It's easy to paint how you feel. But it's harder to say it when someone's staring at you with crossed arms and an angry look on her face.

"I'm sorry," I mumble.

Parents should know it's embarrassing to get in trouble when you have a friend over. "Mary Ann is waiting for me downstairs," I tell them.

"I think we've talked enough for one night," says Dad. He and Mom kiss me good night. But I can tell what they're really thinking is *bad night*.

And I agree. This was a very, very, very bad night.

AT THE WISH POND

I look through the stones on the edge of the wish pond. I'd like to find a wish pebble. The problem is they're never around when you need one.

"Doughnut for your thoughts," says Dad. He sits down next to me and opens a box of chocolate doughnuts with colored sprinkles.

I shake my head. I love doughnuts, but this morning, I'm not in the mood.

Dad puts the box down and picks through the rocks on the edge of the pond.

"What are you looking for?" I ask.

Dad doesn't answer. He keeps picking through the rocks.

"If you're looking for a wish pebble, you might as well give up," I tell him. "They're pretty hard to find."

"No," says Dad. "I'm not looking for a wish pebble." He stops digging through the rocks and looks at me. "I'm looking for the Mallory I know who always works at something until things work out the way she'd like them to."

Dad smiles. "Lately, she's been pretty hard to find."

I kick my toe in the water. "You're not going to find her under a rock."

Dad hands me a doughnut. "I peeked into your room this morning. Mary Ann

129

was still asleep, and your bed was empty.
I thought you might be out here."

I pick a sprinkle off my doughnut.

"Feel like talking?" asks Dad.

I shake my head from side to side.

Dad looks at the pile of stones in my lap.
"Well, since this is a wish pond, I bet you
came out here to make some wishes. Am
I right about that?"

I shake my head up and down.

"Feel like telling me what you plan to wish for?"

"If I tell you, my wishes might not come true."

Dad puts his arm around me and pulls me close to him. "Sweet Potato, it might help to talk about what's bothering you."

I hadn't planned to talk, but everything

that's bothering me starts popping out of my mouth like kernels flying out of the popcorn machine at the movies.

"I wish I was still at my old school with Mary Ann.

"I wish things with Joey were like they were this summer.

"I wish Mom hadn't picked a stupid theme for Fall Festival.

"I wish she hadn't made me invite Mary Ann to see the show.

"I wish things could be like they used to be before Mom was a teacher.

"And what I really wish is that I could make her not mad at me anymore."

"Phew." Dad takes a deep breath. "That's a pretty long list. Got any ideas how you might make some of those wishes come true?"

I shrug.

Dad pulls me closer to him. "Feel like hearing a story?"

I shrug again. I know Dad will tell his story, whether I want to hear it or not.

"Once upon a time there was a little girl," says Dad. "She loved to play with blocks. She used to build all kinds of things out of blocks. She would build houses and schools and boats and even cities out of blocks.

"Now this little girl had an older brother. One day, her brother used her blocks to build a tower. He built a big, tall tower with all the blocks. When he was finished, his tower stood straight and tall, almost as tall as the little girl.

"The little girl must have decided to herself that building a big, tall tower looked like fun because that's what she started to do."

Dad pauses and looks at me. "But she soon found out that building big, tall towers wasn't as easy as it looked. Every time her tower started to get tall, it fell over.

"But the little girl didn't stop building. For weeks, she kept building towers. Every time her tower fell over, she started over again until, finally, she built a big, tall block tower with all of her blocks, just like the one her older brother had built."

Dad is quiet for a minute. He picks up a handful of stones from the edge of the wish pond and starts stacking them one on top of the other, until they topple over.

"Building towers isn't easy. But the little girl stuck with it until she did it." Dad looks at me. "I knew right then and there that this little girl would always keep trying until she accomplished what she set out to do."

I throw a rock in the water. "Are you talking about me?"

Dad nods.

"Now my problems are bigger than building a tower out of blocks."

"And you're bigger now than the little girl in the story," says Dad. "I'm sure if you'll just give yourself and everyone around you a chance, you'll find a way to make things just the way you'd like them to be. You always have, and I know you always will."

Dad stands up and hands me the box of doughnuts. "I'm going home now. Why don't you take a few minutes to think before the day gets started."

After Dad leaves, I take another doughnut out of the box. So much has changed since we moved. Things aren't the way I'd like them to be. Especially things with Mom.

I think about the conversation I had with Mom and Dad last night. Actually, it wasn't a conversation because I didn't do any talking. Mom did it all.

There were things I wanted to say, like I wish she had considered someone's feelings besides her own . . . MINE! But all I did was mumble *I'm sorry*.

And I am sorry. Sorry I was ever born.

I think Mom would be a whole lot happier if she didn't have a daughter at the school where she teaches. Then she could say to people: *Meet my ONLY child Max. He's a bright, happy fifth grader. He plays baseball. He eats frozen meatballs. And he doesn't mind that I teach music at his school.*

I know Mom was really upset last night. Even though part of me is mad at Mom, all of her is mad at me, and I don't like it when she is mad at me.

I tear off a piece of doughnut and toss it into the water.

I wish I could do something so Mom wouldn't be mad anymore.

"MALLORY!" Mom yells from down the street. "COME ON, MARY ANN AND HER MOM ARE LEAVING IN A FEW MINUTES."

I bet Mom wanted to say: *"Pack a bag and you can go with them."*

I stand up and throw the rest of my doughnut into the pond.

I think about what Dad said, about finding a way to make things how I want them to be. But I think no matter what I do, Mom will still be mad at me.

I think the best thing for me to do is to look in the yellow pages this afternoon and see if I can find a new mom.

PART OF A PLAN

When I get to school on Monday morning, I feel like everyone is thinking the same thing: there goes the eggplant who didn't really break her leg.

I walk to my classroom and sit down at my desk.

Pamela is already in her seat. She smiles at me. It looks like a *good-morning-my-mom-told-me-I-had-to-be-nice-to-you-even-though-you-ruined-Fall-Festival* smile.

Mrs. Daily taps Chester. "Class, please

open your science books to chapter five."

I flip to chapter five. Bears. Bears have it easy. They don't have to go to school. They don't have to be in shows. I'd like to be a bear.

"Joey, please read for us," says Mrs. Daily.

Joey reads. "Bears can be found throughout the world. They are large mammals with thick, coarse fur and short tails. Bears walk flat on the soles of their

feet. Black bears, brown bears, and polar bears are three of the most well-known types of bears."

If I were a bear, I'm not sure which kind I'd want to be.

"Sammy, will you please continue," asks Mrs. Daily.

Sammy takes over where Joey left off.

"Bears spend the winter months asleep or in an inactive condition called *hibernation*. They emerge from their caves in the spring, in late March or April."

Now I know what kind of bear I want to be . . . the kind that hibernates.

I could go to sleep now and wake up in March. By then, everybody would forget about the eggplant who didn't really break her leg at Fall Festival . . . especially Mom.

I wonder if there are any caves in Fern Falls.

While I'm busy planning my hibernation, Pamela passes me a note. It says *this concerns you* on the outside. I'm not speaking to Pamela, but when I get a *this-concerns-you* note, I want to read it. I unfold the paper.

Mallory, I have a plan. YOU ARE PART OF THIS PLAN!!!! Meet me under the monkey bars at recess. I'll explain then. I KNOW you will like it. When the bell rings, HURRY! We have a LOT to talk about. YOU HAVE TO COME!
Your friend, Pamela

I can't imagine what Pamela has in mind. I look at her, but she moves her fingers across her lips like she's zipping them shut.

Pamela and I haven't been what you'd call friends since she stole my idea. But still, part of me wants to know what her plan is.

I think about what Dad said to me at the wish pond, about giving other people a chance. Maybe I should give Pamela a chance.

When the recess bell rings, I do *eenie, meenie, miney, mo.* I squeeze my palm and decide to . . . GO.

Pamela is waiting under the monkey bars when I get to the playground.

When I walk over to the monkey bars, Pamela looks at me. She looks nervous.

I feel like I should say something, but I haven't said anything to Pamela for a long time, so I don't know what to say.

Pamela faces me and folds her hands in her lap. "Mallory, your mom seemed pretty upset with you last night."

"So?" I shrug. I don't know why Pamela cares if Mom is mad at me.

"Well, I think I know a way to get her unmad."

"Huh?" I raise my eyebrows. I'd like to find a way to get Mom unmad at me.

"Why don't we ask Mrs. Daily if you can write the next Teacher-of-the-Month column about your mom?"

Pamela leans toward me like she's telling me a secret she doesn't want anyone else to hear. "Since your mom just did Fall Festival, kids will think it's interesting to learn more about her. You can say how sorry you are about what happened, and when she reads it in the paper, she won't be mad anymore."

I consider Pamela's plan.

"Tomorrow is the last day to submit

articles for the next issue," Pamela continues. "Why don't we go talk to Mrs. Daily before recess is over."

Even though I'm still a little mad at Pamela, I think her plan is a good one. "That sounds great. I think it's really nice that you want to help me, but I guess I don't understand why you want to."

I look down at some grass growing under the corner of the monkey bars. "After all, I did ruin Fall Festival."

Pamela picks at a blade of grass. "We all make mistakes. I'm sorry I took your idea for *The Daily News*," she says. "I'd like to be friends."

I didn't think I would ever smile again, but I do. "I'd like to be friends too."

"Do you want to come over to my house after school?" asks Pamela. "You can write your article. I'll help if you want."

I nod my head. "Sure."

"Um, maybe it's not such a good idea," says Pamela.

Uh-oh. I hope we don't stop being friends before we get started. "How come?"

"Well," says Pamela. "My sister Amanda will want to do everything with us. She won't leave us alone long enough to write the article. She can be a real pain sometimes."

"I've got a big brother, and he's always a pain. But I can't believe little sisters can be annoying."

Pamela laughs. "Believe it! I can't believe you didn't know that."

I guess there are lots of things about Pamela I didn't know.

"Hey," I say. "Why don't I bring my purple nail polish to your house, and Amanda can paint her fingernails while we write the article."

"Great idea. Amanda will love that."
Pamela grabs my hand. "We better go talk
to Mrs. Daily before we miss our chance."

We run back to the classroom.

I can't help thinking about what Dad
said: *Sometimes you just have to give people a
chance.* I'm glad I gave one to Pamela.

MOM-OF-THE-MONTH

"It's out!" I scream. I clutch *The Daily News* with one hand and cover my eyes with the other.

Pamela grabs the paper out of my hand. "Open your eyes, silly."

I peek . . . just a little. "Don't you know how hard it is to read your own work?"

Pamela laughs. "That's only when it's bad." She starts reading aloud.

TEACHER-OF-THE-MONTH:
Fern Falls Elementary music
teacher, Mrs. McDonald
by Mallory McDonald (her loving and only
daughter)

   Mrs. McDonald is a new face to
many of the students at Fern Falls
Elementary, but she's not new to
me. She's been my mom for 8¾
years, my entire life.
   When she was a piano teacher at
home, she taught one student at a
time. But now that she's the music
teacher at Fern Falls Elementary,
she teaches lots of students.
   I was really worried when I found
out she was going to be the music
teacher at my school. I thought she
wouldn't have time to be a mom and

a teacher. I thought I was losing a mom, but I realized what I gained was a great music teacher.

She's the world's best music teacher for lots of reasons.

She doesn't laugh at kids who sing off-key. She doesn't ask questions about composers who died a gazillion years ago. But best of all, Mrs. McDonald loves all kids and vegetables equally, even rotten ones (who are very, very, very sorry for any bad behavior and promise to be good from now on).

As a music teacher and a mom, Mrs. McDonald gets an A+. Mrs. McDonald is not only the Teacher-of-the-Month. She's the Mom-of-the-Month too.

Pamela folds the paper closed. "It's great," she says. "Your mom will love it."

I cross my fingers. I hope Pamela is right.

Even though she says she's not, I can tell Mom is still mad at me.

On Saturday, she made me clean out my drawers.

On Sunday, she didn't make peanut butter marshmallow pancakes. She always makes them for me on Sundays, and this Sunday, I got plain old pancakes.

And ever since Fall Festival, she's been calling me by my full name, Mallory Louise McDonald. The only time she calls me by my full name is when she's mad.

I hope Mom likes the article, and I hope she'll really forgive me for ruining Fall Festival. I don't know how I'm going to be able to wait until music class to see if Mom liked my article.

Mrs. Daily taps Chester on the head. "Class, take your seats and open your social studies books to page eighty-seven."

I open my book to a picture of Christopher Columbus.

"It took Christopher Columbus over two months to sail across the ocean with the Nina, the Pinta, and the Santa Maria to get to the New World," says Mrs. Daily.

"It took years to put his plan into place and see it through to completion. So you can see," says Mrs. Daily, "some plans take a very long time to work."

I hope my plan works faster than Christopher Columbus's did.

After social studies, Mrs. Daily says to take out our science books.

Someone knocks on the door.

"Class, please start reading on page sixty-one." She walks outside and shuts the door behind her.

I start reading, but Mrs. Daily cracks the door open. "Mallory, may I see you."

Uh-oh . . . whoever was talking to Mrs. Daily must have been talking about me! What if Mom's not the only one who's mad about Fall Festival? What if it's the principal and I'm in BIG trouble?

I walk outside . . . slowly.

But when I get outside, I'm surprised. It's not the principal . . . it's my mom.

"Mallory, your mother would like to have a word with you." Mrs. Daily winks at Mom then smiles at me. "Your article was excellent," she says.

Mrs. Daily goes back into the classroom.

I wish I could follow her inside. I'm not sure what Mom is doing here. There's a copy of *The Daily News* in her hand. I can't tell if she's happy or mad.

I cross my toes. "Did you like the article?"

Mom puts her arm around me. "What do you say we discuss it over lunch? How does McDonald's sound?"

Mom is taking me out for lunch? I get to go to McDonald's? She knows all McDonalds love McDonald's.

Mom is quiet in the car. When we sit down, I unwrap my cheeseburger and take a bite. But Mom doesn't touch her food.

"Mallory, what you did at the Fall Festival was wrong, and I think you know that."

I nod my head.

"I don't think you'll do anything like that again."

I nod my head again.

"And I know you're sorry that you ruined a special night for a lot of people."

I keep nodding. I hope I don't throw up my cheeseburger from all this nodding.

Mom spreads *The Daily News* on the table and turns to the page with my article on it. "But this is wonderful." She smiles at me.

Phew. I think it's safe to stop nodding. "Mom, I'm sorry I pretended to break my leg. I wish I hadn't ruined the show."

Mom takes a sip of her shake. "Is there anything else you'd like to say?"

Actually, there is. There are a lot of things I'd like to say. I take a deep breath.

"I didn't want you to be the music teacher at my school. I didn't want you to pick the theme you picked for Fall Festival. And I didn't want Mary Ann to come see the show. I tried to tell you, but you didn't listen to anything I had to say."

I feel like I've said enough, but for some reason, I keep going. "It's hard to share your mom with a whole school, especially when you're used to having her to yourself. It's not that being an eggplant was so bad, but I felt like you were spending so much time planning Fall Festival, you barely had time to be my mom. You even gave us frozen meatballs. You never gave us frozen meatballs before you were a teacher."

Mom is quiet for a minute. "Mallory, just because I gave you frozen meatballs doesn't mean I love you less. And I'll try to listen to what you have to say from now on. But sometimes things happen that you might not like. When they do, you might find they're not all that bad if you just give them a chance."

I take a sip of my shake. I think about Pamela. I gave her a chance, and I'm glad I did. Maybe Mom is right. "I'll try," I tell her.

Mom looks at me in a happy way, like she just ate an extra-salty french fry.

"Mallory, I'm proud of you. You did a good job telling me how you feel and you wrote a wonderful article. Sometimes we all have a tough time saying what's on our minds, and you expressed yourself beautifully."

Thinking about what Mom said makes me feel happy. I wonder if this is how Vincent Van Gogh felt when he painted.

Expressionism is starting to make more sense to me.

"Mom, there's something else I want to say."

Mom puts down her milk shake, and looks at me like what I have to say is important to her. "What's that?" she asks.

"I'm getting used to Fern Falls Elementary. I even think there are some fun parts to having you teach at the same school."

"Oh yeah?" Mom raises an eyebrow. "Which parts do you think are fun?"

I take a big bite of my cheeseburger. "The eating lunch at McDonald's part." I lean forward and whisper so no one but Mom can hear me. "It's a lot more fun than eating in that stinky cafeteria."

Mom looks around the restaurant and leans forward. "I think the cafeteria is stinky too. But I'll tell you a secret if you promise not to tell."

I nod.

"I keep a secret stash of candy bars in my desk. Sometimes I just need to eat something sweet to get that cafeteria smell out of my nose. You're welcome to stop by my room if you think a little bit of candy might help you too."

Going to lunch at McDonald's, access to a secret candy stash . . . having Mom as a teacher might be even better than I thought it would be.

"Sounds like a plan," I tell Mom.

We smile and dip our french fries in the ketchup cup at the same time.

HAPPY HALLOWEEN!

Someone sits down on my bed and rubs my back.

"Guess who?" says a voice.

Even though I'm covered with covers, I don't have to guess. I know it's Mom.

She tickles my back. "Rise and shine, Sleepyhead. It's Halloween!" Then she whispers in my ear. "I have a Halloween surprise for you. Candy corn pancakes . . .

your favorite!"

I sit up. "I have a surprise for you too. I'm not going to be a witch this year."

Mom is quiet for a minute. "But you're always a witch on Halloween. If you're not going to be a witch, what are you going to be?"

I smile at Mom. "That's another surprise."

When I finish my pancakes, I ask Mom if I can borrow the aluminum foil. I take it into my room and close the door. I get out paints and poster board and string and scissors and glue. Joey and Pamela are coming over, and we're making Halloween costumes.

After I set everything up, I go outside to wait for my friends.

When they arrive, we go into my room.

Max follows us. "What's going on in here?"

"You'll find out soon enough." I lock my door.

"So what do we do?" asks Joey. "I've never made my own costume."

Pamela looks through all the art supplies on the floor of my room. "Actually, neither have I." She smiles at me. "Mallory, you have to tell us where to start."

I smile at both of them. I know exactly where to start.

We spend the morning cutting, pasting, and coloring.

When Joey and Pamela and I finish gluing the last pieces on our costumes, we punch holes in the tops, tie strings through the holes, and slip them over our heads.

I spin around so they can see me. "What do you think?"

"I think no one else in Fern Falls will be dressed like us," says Joey.

"I think we're ready," says Pamela. We all nod and march into the kitchen to model our costumes for Mom and Max.

Mom gasps when she sees us. Even Max looks like he's impressed.

"What do you think?" I ask.

Mom grins. "Three Musketeers, very clever."

Max walks around us in a circle like he's a costume inspector. "Not bad," he says to Joey and Pamela. He stops in front of me. "Pretty good costume. Just try not to break a leg while you're wearing it."

Everybody laughs. Even Mom.

She takes her camera out of the drawer. "Get together, guys."

We put our arms around each other.

Mom says, "Say Happy Halloween," and snaps our picture.

"See you tonight," I tell Joey and Pamela.

They're going home and coming back to my house tonight to trick-or-treat. "Six o'clock sharp and don't be late. We have a lot of houses to go to!"

After they leave, Mom hands me an envelope. "This came for you this morning."

It's from Mary Ann! She wrote *HAPPY HALLOWEEN!* on the outside in big black and orange letters. I take her letter to my room and open it.

Dear Mallory,

HAPPY HALLOWEEN!

What are you going to be for Halloween this year?

Even though we won't be together, I'm going to be a witch, just like always. BUT HALLOWEEN WON'T BE THE SAME THIS YEAR!

Not without you or Cheeseburger. I won't have anybody to glue on fake black fingernails with. I won't have anybody to trade candy with. I won't even have a cat to go with my costume. Nobody will be able to say, "Which witch are you?"

Here's a Halloween poem for you:
Boo-Hoo! Boo-Hoo! Boo-Hoo!
Halloween won't be the same without you.
Hugs, hugs, hugs!
Kisses, kisses, kisses!
Mary Ann

I reread Mary Ann's letter. Then I take out my Halloween scrapbook and paste Mary Ann's letter in it. I leave enough room on the page to put in the picture Mom took of Joey, Pamela, and me.

This Halloween will be different from all my other Halloweens.

I used to go trick-or-treating with Mary Ann. Then we'd go back to her house and put our candy in a big bowl and share it all until it was gone. Some years, we got enough candy to last until Christmas.

This Halloween, I'm trick-or-treating with Joey and Pamela . . . *and* Winnie and Max are coming too. Max has never trick-or-treated with me, but when he heard that Winnie was coming, he decided to come along.

When we finish, we're meeting at the wish pond for a party. Joey says Halloween at the wish pond is a Wish Pond Road tradition.

I think about the wish pond. I've spent a lot of time there lately making a lot of wishes. And I've noticed something: sometimes my wishes come true, sometimes they don't, and sometimes they take a while to work.

I guess what Mom says is true: you have to give things a chance . . . even wishes.

I pull a sheet of paper out of my desk drawer.

Dear Mary Ann,
HAPPY HALLOWEEN TO YOU TOO!
I know you will be a very cute witch. Cheeseburger and I will both miss being part of the costume. You are right about one thing—HALLOWEEN WON'T BE THE

SAME THIS YEAR . . . not without you!

Believe it or not, I'm not going to be a witch this year.

At first, I thought I would be a witch because I'm always a witch with you. But I decided to try something different.

So you'll never guess what I'm going to be—a Three Musketeer. Not the sword fighter kind, the candy bar kind. Joey, Pamela, and I are going trick-or-treating together as The Three Musketeers.

It was my idea. When I told Joey about it, he said he wanted to go as a soccer player. So I told Joey that something was bugging me. I told him that I felt like he only wanted to be my friend some of the time, not all of the time.

I even told him that Max said he was just my "street friend." (Max says a "street friend" is someone who lives on your street and only wants to be friends at home.)

Joey said it was silly that Max said that. (Most of the stuff Max says is silly.)

Joey said friends can be different and still be friends. Then he said the more he thought about the candy bar idea, the more he liked it and to count him in.

When I told Pamela the idea, she said she LOVED IT! She even told Mrs. Daily about it (she made her promise not to tell anyone), and Pamela told her it was my idea.

Mrs. Daily told me she thought it was a delightfully sweet idea!

That's all for now. I have to go help Dad hang Halloween decorations in our yard. HAVE FUN TONIGHT! EAT LOTS OF CANDY!

I'm going to even though I know what Mom is going to say: "Don't eat too many sweets. You don't want to get a tummy ache before you go to bed."

But I know exactly what I'm going to tell her.

I'm going to tell her not to worr . . . because I like sweet endings!

Ha! Ha! Ha! Get the joke? Sweets. Sweet endings.

Happy, Happy, Happy Halloween!!!

Extra, Extra, Extra Big Huge Hugs and Kisses,

Mallory

CLASS PICTURES

Oh yeah! I almost forgot . . . next week we're taking class pictures and I can't decide what to wear. Mary Ann and I used to always help each other pick out just the right outfits, but since she's not here this year, I asked a few other people.

Dad said I should ask Mom. He said he's "no good" in the *picking-clothes* department. Mom said as long as I smile and say, "Cheese," I'll be fine. But Mom knows I always say, "Cheeseburger," when I take a picture.

Max said I should wear a paper bag over my head. Joey said he had no idea what I should wear. Winnie said it wouldn't matter, and Pamela said we should ask Mrs. Daily.

None of these people were any help at all. But maybe you can be. What do you think I should wear?

Me in bell bottoms
and a hippie top

Me in a mini
skirt and a
turtle neck

Me in jeans
and a poncho

Me in boots
and a sweater
dress

It is so hard to pick just the right outfit
for a class picture. Thanks so, so, so much
for your help!

The illustrator wishes to thank the St. Vincent Ferrer class of 2009!

A partial reproduction of the painting, "Still Life: Vase with Twelve Sunflowers" (Bayerische Staatsgemäldesammlungen, Neue Pinakothek, Munich) by Vincent van Gogh is reflected on page 37.

Darby Creek
A division of Lerner Publishing Group, Inc.
241 First Avenue North
Minneapolis, MN 55401 USA

For reading levels and more information, look up this title at www.lernerbooks.com.

Library of Congress Cataloging-in-Publication Data

Friedman, Laurie B.,
    Back to school, Mallory / by Laurie Friedman; illustrations by Tamara Schmitz.
        p.   cm.
    Summary: After moving, eight-year-old Mallory struggles with being new at school, especially because her mother is now the music teacher and director of the third grade play.
    ISBN 978-1-57505-658-6 (lib. bdg. : alk. paper)
    ISBN 978-1-57505-841-2 (EB pdf)
    [1. Moving, Household—Fiction. 2. First day of school—Fiction. 3. Schools—Fiction. 4. Family life—Fiction.] I. Schmitz, Tamara, ill. II. Title.
PZ7.F897738ac 2004
[Fic]—dc22   2003018043

To my parents, who perfected the art of loving
individually. And to my sisters, who made growing up fun!
With all my heart,
L.B.F.

Laurie – you stole my dedication!
To MY parents, who astoundingly raised six!
Thanks for always providing me with an art studio.
Love,
T

by Laurie Friedman
illustrations by Tamara Schmitz

MINNEAPOLIS

CONTENTS

A WORD FROM MALLORY

Fact: You don't get to choose your brother or your bedtime.

I know. I'm Mallory McDonald. Age 8¾ plus 1 month. And I got stuck with a brother and a bedtime I never would have chosen myself.

First, let me tell you about my bedtime. It's 8:30. My brother Max, who is 10, gets to stay up until 9:30.

And a later bedtime isn't all Max gets. He's getting a dog! You're probably thinking that's good news, that dogs are cute and fun. Even though I'm a cat person, I don't disagree. But the thing is, ever since Mom and Dad said Max could get a dog, that's all anyone in this house ever talks about.

6

Take last night at dinner, for example. When I told Mom I needed new sneakers, she said we should wait, that we wouldn't want the dog to chew up a new pair of shoes. She and Dad and Max laughed. But not me. It made my toes hurt just thinking about it.

So this morning, I tried talking to my parents. "I don't know why we're getting a dog. We already have a cat—Cheeseburger. Remember her?"

But I don't think my parents remembered my cat or me because right in the middle of my talk, Max barged in with a book about dogs, and faster than you can say flea powder, my parents were talking to Max like I wasn't even in the room.

Fact: Ever since my parents said Max could get a dog, things in this house haven't been so good for me.

Another fact: Once we actually get the dog, I'm scared they're going to get a whole lot worse.

MALLORY MARCHES

I started a new club.

It's called SABGD. That's short for Sisters Against Brothers Getting Dogs.

Right now, I'm the president and the only member of the club, but soon things will change. When other girls see how much attention their brothers get when their parents say, *"You can get a dog,"* they will want to join my club too.

I will teach club members to protest.

I will teach club members to speak out.

I will teach club members to march, which is what I'm doing right now.

I march into the kitchen with my cat, Cheeseburger, and pass out flyers to Mom and Dad. "Mallory McDonald, founding member of Sisters Against Brothers Getting Dogs, has something to say," I shout through my megaphone.

Mom and Dad put down their coffee cups and stare at me.

I put down my megaphone and start reading.

10 Reasons Why I, Mallory McDonald, Think Max should <u>NOT</u> get a dog.

<u>Reason #1</u>: Dogs eat a lot. Not only dog food... shoes too!

<u>Reason #2</u>: Dogs drink a lot. They drink out of toilets. If you kiss Max's dog, it will be the same thing as drinking out of a toilet.

<u>Reason #3</u>: Dogs dig a lot. Max's dog will dig in our yard and in our neighbors' yards. No one on our street will like us if Max gets a dog.

<u>Reason #4</u>: Dogs bark a lot. If Max gets a dog, it will bark all night and we will never get a good night's sleep.

<u>Reason #5</u>: Dogs poop a lot. In the winter, our backyard will

look like a giant chocolate chip cookie.

Reason # 6: Dogs chase away important people, like garbagemen and paperboys.

Reason # 7: Dogs need a lot of attention. They want everybody to look at them and pet them and say how cute they are... all of the time!

Reason # 8: Dogs make people say stupid things. Max will start saying stupid things like, "The dog ate my homework."

Reason # 9: Dogs have to be taken care of. MAX WILL NOT DO THIS! You will be the one taking care of the dog!

Reason # 10: We already have a pet—CHEESEBURGER! Her feelings will be very, very, very hurt if we get another pet!

I finish reading my flyer and wait. I'm waiting for Mom and Dad to say, *"Mallory, that makes sense. You're right. We're wrong. We won't get a dog for Max."*

But that's not what they say. Dad tells me to sit down. "Mallory, I'm not sure I understand why you're so upset about Max getting a dog," he says.

"Lots of reasons," I tell Dad. "I just gave you ten of them."

Dad reads from the list. "I'm not worried about the eating, drinking, digging, barking, and pooping. That's what dogs do."

"What about number six?" I ask Dad. "What about chasing away garbagemen and paperboys? What are you going to do when we have garbage piled up to the roof, and you don't know what's going on in the world?"

Dad smiles. "That's a good point. We'll keep the dog inside when the garbagemen and the paperboy show up."

"What about seven? Your hand will get tired from petting a dog *all* the time."

Dad laughs.

I wave my list in his face. "How about eight? Aren't you worried that Max won't do his homework because he'll be too busy playing with a dog?"

Dad shakes his head.

I point my finger at reason number nine. "If we get a dog, Max won't take care of it. You and Mom will have to do all the work. Did you think about that?" I ask Dad.

Dad nods. "Max knows he's responsible for taking care of this dog."

"Well, what about ten? Aren't you worried about Cheeseburger?"

Dad looks me straight in the eye. "I'm

not worried about one, two, three, four, five, six, seven, eight, or even nine. But yes, ten concerns me."

Finally, Dad is starting to see my point, and it's about time.

I cover Cheeseburger's ears. "Ten should concern you. How do you think Cheeseburger will feel if we get a dog?"

"Cheeseburger isn't the one I'm worried about," says Dad. "It might take some time, but Cheeseburger will get used to a new dog." Dad smiles at me. "Sweet Potato, getting a dog will be fun."

Getting a dog will be fun for *some* people, but not *all* people. I cross my arms. "Getting a dog will be fun for Max," I tell Dad.

Mom gives Dad an *I'll-take-it-from-here* look. "Mallory, you need to change your attitude. Getting a dog will be fun for our

whole family. Dogs are so lovable, and
whatever dog we get will love everybody in
our family," Mom says.

I pick up a flyer and wave it at Mom and
Dad. "Didn't you read this?"

"I'd like to read it if you don't mind,"
says a voice behind me.

Max plucks my flyer
out of my hand. He
reads it, then crushes it
into a ball, and tosses
it in the trash. "I *won't*
say the dog ate my
homework. And I *will*
take care of it!"

Mom pours herself
some more coffee.
"Let's all calm down,"
she says.

"Mom, Dad," says

Max. "I promised I would take care of this dog, and I will. Mallory has a cat. I'm getting a dog. Fair is fair."

"I didn't *get* a cat," I remind Max. "I found a cat, and I got to keep her."

Max must be the only brother on the planet who doesn't understand the difference between rescuing an abandoned animal and getting a pet when you already have one.

Max shrugs. "If you ask me, it doesn't matter how you got your pet. It just matters that you have one, and now, I'll have one too. Right, Dad?"

"I think we'll all enjoy having a dog," says Dad. He puts his coffee cup in the sink. Then he looks at me. "We're getting a dog, and that's final. We'll start our search at the pet store on Saturday."

Dad picks up his car keys. "See you all later. I have to go to work."

I wait until I hear his car pull out of the driveway. Then I pick up my megaphone. "No fair! No fair! No fair!" I shout through the little opening.

Max looks at me like I'm a dirt stain on his baseball pants. Then he makes rings around his ear with his finger like I'm crazy. "What a weirdo."

I ignore Max. Thoughts of other girls who, one day, might have to go through what I'm going through fill my brain.

I pick up Cheeseburger and march across the kitchen. "Sisters Against Brothers Getting Dogs!" I shout through my megaphone.

"Mallory, that's enough," says Mom.

"This march has just begun," I tell her.

I march around the kitchen table and

into the dining room. "SISTERS AGAINST BROTHERS GETTING DOGS!" I chant.

But when I march back into the kitchen, my march is stopped by a blockade . . . a mom blockade.

Mom takes my megaphone and holds it up to her mouth. "There's only one place you need to march, young lady, and that's straight to your room!"

LIFE'S NOT FAIR!

"No peeking!" I pull Mom and Dad by their hands and sit them down on my bed. I've been waiting all week for Saturday to get here, and now that it's here, I don't want to spoil the surprise. "OK," I say. "Open your eyes!"

When my parents open their eyes, they look very surprised.

"Mallory, why are all your scrapbooks on the floor of your room instead of on the shelf in your closet?" Mom asks me.

"It's Scrapbook Day!" I tell her. I put Cheeseburger in Mom's lap and pick up a pink scrapbook with the word *Kindergarten* on the cover. "You and Dad and I are going to spend the day looking at all of my old scrapbooks."

Dad raises an eyebrow. "Mallory, today we're going to . . . "

But before Dad can finish his sentence, I plop down on the bed between Mom and Dad and open my *Kindergarten* scrapbook to a picture of me with a big bow in my hair and a little backpack on wheels. "This is me on my first day of school."

Mom looks over my shoulder at Dad.

I start turning pages. I show them a picture of me eating animal crackers at snack time and a picture of me pushing a shopping cart on a class field trip to the grocery store.

Dad clears his throat. "Mallory . . . "

I close my *Kindergarten* scrapbook. "Now we're going to look at my *First Grade* scrapbook." I reach for a thick, blue book with alphabet letters on it, but when I do, a pair of black sneakers are blocking my way. "Move it," I tell Max. But he doesn't.

"Dad, when are we going to the pet store?" asks Max. "It's Saturday, and you said we could look for a dog today."

I reach around Max's leg to get my *First Grade* scrapbook. "Mom and Dad can't go today. It's Scrapbook Day."

"Scrapbook Day?" Max laughs. "We're going to the pet store. Right, Dad?"

I ignore Max, open my scrapbook, and point to a picture of me carrying a lunch box. "Dad, isn't this a cute picture?"

But Dad isn't looking at the picture. He looks at Mom. Then he looks at me.

"Mallory, I love looking at all these pictures of you, but we had planned to go to the pet store today. What do you say we do Scrapbook Day tomorrow?"

I turn the page. "Here I am writing on the chalkboard."

Dad puts his arm around me. "Sweet Potato, you need to put the scrapbooks away. We're going to the pet store."

I cross my arms. "You and Mom and Max planned to go to the pet store, but nobody asked me if that's what I wanted to do."

"I'm sure we'll all have fun," says Mom.

She puts Cheeseburger on my bed and starts picking up scrapbooks. "We'll help you clean up, and then we'll go."

"Great," says Max. He grabs a scrapbook and throws it into my closet.

It lands on a pile of shoes. "Mom! Tell Max to be careful with my stuff."

"Max!" Mom gives Max a stern look.

Max shrugs his shoulders and gives Mom a *what-did-I-do-wrong* look. But I know he knows what he did wrong.

"I'll finish here," says Mom. "Why don't you two go outside for a few minutes."

"Is it OK if I go next door and see if Joey wants to come to the pet store with us?" Max asks Dad. "Since he has a dog, he could be a big help."

"I think that's a fine idea," says Dad. "Why don't you and Mallory go together."

Max walks toward the front door.

I scoop up Cheeseburger and follow Max outside. I have to run-walk to keep up with him. Joey is my friend, not Max's! Max even says that living next door to Joey is the worst part of living on Wish Pond Road.

Just because Max is getting a dog and Joey has one doesn't mean Max can steal my friends. "Since when do you care what Joey thinks?" I ask Max.

Max pushes the Winstons' doorbell. "Joey is a dog expert."

"That's not fair!" I say to Max. "You can't just take my friends."

"Life's not fair," says Max like he's an old, smart person talking to a young, stupid one. Then he starts laughing.

When Joey opens the front door, Max stops laughing and starts explaining. "The thing is, I don't know what kind of dog I want to get. Want to help me pick?"

Joey smiles. "Sure! But you'll know the right dog when you see it." Joey pats his dog, Murphy. "I knew the minute I saw Murphy that he was for me."

Max nods his head like that makes sense to him, like it's something that only a kid getting a dog could understand.

"Come in," says Joey. "Let me put on my sweatshirt and we'll go." Max follows Joey down the hall. I go into the Winstons' kitchen. Winnie is at the table peeling an orange.

"What do you want?" she says without looking up.

"Max is getting a dog. He came over to see if Joey would go to the pet store with us. Want to come too?" I ask.

Winnie pops a piece of orange into her mouth and chews it slowly. "I wouldn't go to a pet store if it were the last place on the planet," she says when she's done chewing.

I sit down at the table holding
Cheeseburger. Now that Max is getting a
dog, Winnie and I have a lot in common.
"So what's it like having a brother with a
dog?"

Winnie makes a face like she's about to
get a shot. "Get ready."

"For what?"

Winnie raises an eyebrow. "When Joey
got Murphy, everybody treated that dog
like he was the president."

I think about all the attention Max has
already gotten, and he hasn't even gotten a
dog yet. "It must have been pretty bad," I
say to Winnie.

Winnie laughs. "That wasn't the worst
part. The worst part is *having* a dog. Soon
you'll step in things that make a used wad
of gum seem like a birthday present. And
your clothes will be covered in dog hairs."

She picks one off her shirt and hands it to me.

"It's awful," continues Winnie. "I refuse to even say the word *D-O-G*. If you think your life is bad now, just wait."

I pick up Cheeseburger. "Thanks," I say. "I have to be going."

"Watch where you step," she says as I'm leaving.

When I get home, I go into my room, shut the door, and pull out my *Cheeseburger*

scrapbook. I snuggle up on my bed with her. "Want to see your baby book?" I ask her.

I open the first page and tell Cheeseburger the story of how I found her.

"Once upon a time, there was a teeny, tiny kitten that lost her mother. The kitten wandered into the yard of a sweet, little girl."

I show Cheeseburger a picture of me holding her when she was a baby.

"The little girl put out a bowl of milk and some food. She thought the kitten would leave and go look for her mother, but the kitten stayed. So the little girl took the kitten inside and made a bed for her on her pillow."

I show Cheeseburger a picture of her sleeping on top of my bed in my old house.

"The little girl thought the kitten was happy there. But just to be sure, she went

next door to get her lifelong best friend, who agreed that the kitten must love her a lot. Together, they convinced the little girl's mother to let her keep the kitten."

I show Cheeseburger a picture of Mary Ann and me holding her.

"The little girl named her kitten Cheeseburger after her favorite food, and they lived happily ever after . . . until the little girl grew up, moved to a new town, left behind her old best friend, and tragically learned that her older brother was going to get a dog."

I close Cheeseburger's baby book and rub her back. "Max is right about one thing," I tell her. "Life's not fair."

KING MAX

"Welcome to the Pet Palace!" A lady carrying a scepter and wearing a crown with the name *Patsy* on it greets us at the door. "What can I do for you?"

Dad puts his arm around Max. "This young man is looking for a dog."

Patsy picks up a paper crown and a magic marker. "What's this young man's name?"

When Dad introduces Max, Patsy writes *Max* on the front of the paper crown and plops it on Max's head. "At the Pet Palace, pets rule, and so do our customers."

Patsy points her scepter to the back of the store. "To the dog kingdom!"

If you ask me, Max is too old to wear a crown and too young to be a king, but I follow them to the dog kingdom.

Max grins at Joey as we pass through the fish kingdom and the bird kingdom. "I can't wait to get a dog," he says to Joey.

"Yeah," says Joey. "We're going to have so much fun playing with our dogs."

Just thinking about Max and

Joey playing with their dogs does sound like fun . . . *fun that doesn't include me.* A week ago, Max and Joey barely spoke to each other, and now they're practically best friends.

Mom said we would *all* have fun at the pet store, but so far, I'm not having such a good time. When we pass through the cat kingdom, I stop and pick up a box of cat claw polish. I tug on Mom's sleeve. "Mom, can I please get this? Please!"

I read Mom the little poem on the side of the box:

A color for each day of the week
So your cat will have lovely claws.
With Color Me Happy Polish Kit,
Your cat will have mighty fine paws!

Mom looks at the box in my hands.

"Mallory, we bought a new collar for Cheeseburger last week. Today we're here to look at dogs." She puts the polish back on the shelf. "We can get polish another day." Mom walks toward the dog kingdom.

I follow her. I know I'm not getting polish today. But here's what else I'm not getting: How come Max is getting *everything* he wants, and I'm not getting *anything* I want?

I start to tap Mom on the shoulder so I can explain how she could make this trip to the pet store fun for *everybody,* but Patsy taps me on the shoulder with her scepter.

"Over here," she says. Patsy opens a cage filled with furry puppies, takes one out, and hands it to Max. "For you, King Max."

Max rolls the puppy around in his hands. I didn't want Max to get a dog, but the one he's holding is so little and cute, I could see myself liking her. I could even see Cheeseburger liking her. Maybe they could become best friends, like Mary Ann and me. Maybe getting a dog won't be so bad.

I walk over to Max and rub the puppy's back. "We should get this dog," I say to him. "She's so little and cute."

"I don't want a little, cute dog. I want

a big dog." Max hands the puppy back to Patsy. I watch while she puts the dog back into the cage.

"I think that dog would make a great pet," I say to Max.

"Maybe you think that dog would make a great pet, but I don't." Max pushes his crown on top of his head. "And this is going to be my dog."

I think Max is taking this king stuff way too seriously.

"Mom said this dog will love everybody in our family. So everybody in our family ought to get to help decide what kind of dog we get."

Max ignores me and keeps looking inside cages.

"How about this dog?" I say, pointing to a white, fluffy dog.

Max looks at the white, fluffy dog. "I don't want a white, fluffy dog." Max walks up and down the rows of cages filled with dogs. He stops in front of each one, then shakes his head like none of the dogs are quite right.

"Mom, Dad," says Max. "I just don't see a dog here that I want."

"Remember what I told you," says Joey. "You'll know the right dog when you see it."

I give Mom and Dad a *parents-not-Joey-are-supposed-to-know-best* look. "Mom, Dad, you know how you always make us try new foods? You tell us we won't know what we like unless we try it. I think it's the same thing with dogs."

I point to the white fluffy dog. "Max won't know if he likes this dog unless he tries it."

Max rolls his eyes, like that's the dumbest thing he's ever heard. "Joey said I would know when I see the right dog, and I don't."

Dad puts his arm around Max. "What else can you show us?" he asks Patsy.

Patsy walks around the dog kingdom looking inside the cages. "At the Pet Palace, we pride ourselves on having something for everyone, but I don't think we have what your son is looking for," Patsy tells Dad.

Max hangs his head. His crown falls off.

Patsy picks it up and pushes it back down on top of his hair. "How about a pet pig? If you feed them right, they get huge. I had one that got so big, it won a blue ribbon at the state fair."

Max looks disappointed. In a way, I feel sorry for him. I know how sad I would be if I didn't have Cheeseburger.

Suddenly, Patsy's eyes light up. "I've got it!" She points her scepter to the cat kingdom. "How about a kitten? You can even pretend like it's a dog, and soon you'll love it so much, you'll forget you ever wanted a dog."

"That's a great idea!" I say. "Patsy doesn't have a dog you want, so get a cat. Cheeseburger will have a playmate."

Max looks at me like I asked him to stick his head in the toilet. "I'm not getting a cat. Cats are boring. I want a dog."

"Cats aren't boring." Dad looks in Max's direction. "But we did come here to get a dog. Maybe we better do a little more looking," he says to Patsy.

Dad is right. We should do a little more looking . . . for a new brother!

Max didn't even consider the kind of dog I wanted to get! He said cats are boring! I'm glad Cheeseburger wasn't here to hear this. I'm sorry I ever felt sorry for Max!

Patsy sighs. "I wish I had something for you. We like to keep our customers happy." Then she waves her scepter like she's casting a magic spell. "I'll tell you what. I have a friend who has a farm a few hours north of here. He has a litter of puppies that he's trying to find nice homes for. Why don't I give you his phone number."

Dad nods. "That would be great."

Patsy writes the phone number down on a piece of paper and hands it to Dad. "Give him a call and see if you can take a ride up there tomorrow. Maybe those puppies will be more like what you had in mind."

Dad folds the slip of paper Patsy gave him and puts it in his pocket. "Thanks for your help," says Dad.

Patsy tips her crown. "When it comes to

pets, Patsy knows best. Now, hurry back to the Pet Palace. Once you get your pet, we've got everything you'll need to make his home seem like a kingdom."

Then she smiles at us. "Good luck, King Max. I have a good feeling about this."

Max grins. "Me too."

"Me three," says Dad.

"Me four," says Mom.

"Me five," says Joey.

Everybody looks at me. "Me six," I mumble. But the only feeling I have is that I liked Max better before he was crowned king.

MAX'S DAY

"Welcome to Skyline Farm." Farmer Frank shakes Dad's hand as we get out of the van. He looks at Max. "You must be the young man looking for a dog."

Max nods his head.

"Excellent!" Farmer Frank slaps Max on the back. "I bet you're in a hurry to see the cute little critters."

Maybe Max is in a hurry to see the cute little critters, but I'm in a hurry to see my best friend. I tug on Mom's sleeve. "When will Mary Ann be here?"

Mom looks at her watch and smiles. "Mary Ann's house is about an hour from here. Her mom said they would get here as early as possible."

I still can't believe Mom called Mary Ann's mom. I think back to last night.

I went into Mom and Dad's room, and explained to them that ever since they said Max could get a dog, I haven't felt like a very important part of this family.

Dad said I am a super important part of this family, and Mom said she had a super idea. That's when she called Mary Ann's mom to see if they would meet us here today. Mom said she knew today would be special for Max, and she wanted it to be special for me too.

Having Mary Ann here will make today extra special for me!

I throw my arms around Mom and hug her. "Thanks again for inviting Mary Ann to meet us." Mom kisses my forehead, then points down the dirt road that leads to the farm. "Look who I see."

A blue van is coming our way. "It's Mary Ann!" I shout.

"Great," mumbles Max. "I can't wait to see Birdbrain."

I know Max isn't excited to see my lifelong best friend, but I am. Ever since we moved to Fern Falls, I hardly ever get to see Mary Ann.

Mary Ann's mom pulls her van to a stop in front of us, and Mary Ann hops out.

"We're here! We're here! We're here! I thought we'd never get here!" She hugs me. Then she looks around like she's looking for something and she can't find it.

"Where are the puppies?" Mary Ann asks.

"Right this way." Farmer Frank motions us to follow him through a barn.

I follow Farmer Frank, but I can't believe Mary Ann. She hasn't seen me for exactly one month, two weeks, four days, and six hours, and she hardly even said hello. My own best friend is more interested in a puppy she doesn't even know than in me.

I pull on Mary Ann's elbow. "Puppies can be pretty boring," I whisper in her ear.

Then I hold my nose. "And kind of stinky too. Let's go play while Max picks one."

I wait for Mary Ann to say, *"Sure! Let's go play! That sounds like a lot more fun than looking at boring, stinky puppies."* But that's not what she says.

"Look!" Mary Ann points to a small pen behind the barn.

"Say hello to the puppies," says Farmer Frank.

He unlatches the gate to the pen. "The puppies are only eight weeks old. They're still little, so you have to handle 'em carefully."

"C'mon." I tug on Mary Ann's sleeve. But Mary Ann doesn't move. She has a look on her face that people get in cartoons when they're falling in love. And Mary Ann isn't the only one with that look on her face.

Mom, Dad, Max, Joey, even Mary Ann's mom have it too. They're all staring at the puppies like they've been bitten by a love bug.

"C'mon in." Farmer Frank gestures to us to follow him.

Dad motions for Max to go first.

When Max walks into the pen, the puppies scamper to his feet. Max rubs their backs. "Wow, they're so cute. It's going to be hard to choose one."

"Pick 'em up and see which one you fancy," Farmer Frank says to Max.

Max starts picking up puppies. He picks up a brown one, then a black one, then a white one, and then a brown one with a white patch of fur around one eye. Max looks from puppy to puppy. "This might take a while."

"It's a big decision," says Dad. "Take your time."

"C'mon." I try to pull Mary Ann away from the puppies. "Let's go look around the farm."

"Let's stay here," says Mary Ann. "Picking a puppy is a lot more exciting than looking around a farm." Mary Ann starts jumping up and down again. "I can't wait to see which puppy Max picks."

I look at the puppy Max is holding. I try to guess which one he's going to pick. I know which one I would pick, but I know it won't be the same one Max will pick. Even though we're brother and sister, we never seem to like the same things.

Mom points to the little brown puppy with the white patch of fur around his eye. He's licking Max's hand. "Look Max, I think that puppy likes you."

Max rubs his back.

Joey smiles. "He likes you a lot."

I know Mom said this puppy would love everybody in our family, but if it's Max's dog, I wonder if it will love me too.

While Max is deciding which puppy to pick, I do what I always do when I want something to happen and I'm not sure it's going to. I pretend like I'm at the wish pond on my street and have found a wish pebble. I make a wish. *I wish Max will pick a puppy that will like me too.* I pretend to throw my wish pebble in the wish pond so my wish will come true.

"Hey," says Max. "This puppy really does like me." The brown puppy is licking Max's face.

Max hugs the puppy. "I know this is the puppy for me."

Joey grins. "I told you you'd know when you found the right one."

"That's a good choice," says Farmer

Frank. "That puppy is the smartest and fastest of all the puppies. I've seen a lot of dogs, and that one's a real champ."

Farmer Frank pulls a sheet of paper out of his back pocket and hands it to Max.

"Here are some instructions on how to take care of your new dog. But just remember: love your dog, feed your dog, walk your dog, and be consistent. Dogs like routine."

"Don't worry, I'll take really good care of him," says Max.

"I'm sure you will," says Farmer Frank. He and Dad talk for a few minutes. Then Farmer Frank waves good-bye.

Everyone crowds around Max and his new puppy. Mom starts taking pictures.

Mary Ann's mom rubs the puppy's back. "What are you going to name him?"

Mary Ann tickles the puppy's tummy. "Does he get to sleep in your room?"

Joey scratches behind the puppy's ears. "Do you want me to help you train him?"

Mary Ann kisses the puppy on his nose. "Oh, he's so, so, so cute! You're so, so, so lucky you're getting a puppy," Mary Ann says to me like I'm the one getting the puppy.

But I feel like this is Max's puppy, not mine. I feel like today was extra special for Max, but I don't feel like it was extra special for me. Even having my best friend here didn't help.

Dad smiles at the puppy in Max's arms like it's a new baby. "We can go to the pet store tonight and get everything he needs."

"I can't wait to take him home," says Max.

Home. I think about Max taking his new puppy home. I don't know what home will be like with Max's new puppy, but one thing's for sure—life at 17 Wish Pond Road will never be the same.

IN THE DOGHOUSE

I slam my door. Then I open it and slam it again . . . harder this time. I'm waiting for someone to say, *"Mallory, quit slamming your door."* But no one says a word.

I open my door and slam it shut as hard as I can. I don't think putting a dog in time-out for chewing up my favorite fuzzy duck slippers and knocking over my Purple

Passion nail polish is, as Mom says, *"out of line."*

I am mad. I am misunderstood. I am stuck in my room for what Mom calls *"unacceptable behavior."*

Even though I'm not too happy that Mary Ann practically ignored me on the farm, I do the only thing any girl in my position could do. I take out a sheet of paper and start a letter to my best friend.

Dear Mary Ann,

Do you know what it means when someone says you're in the doghouse?

It means you're in big, big, big trouble. And right now, mom says I'm in the doghouse. If you ask me, mom is right. I am in the doghouse...I LIVE in a doghouse!

It has been exactly five days since

max got his dog, and all anyone in this house talks about anymore is max's dog!

max's dog is so cute. max's dog is so sweet. max's dog is so smart.

max's dog! max's dog! max's dog! max's dog doesn't even have a name yet. (He will probably grow up thinking his name is "max's dog.")

When people are not talking about max's dog, they are playing with him or petting him or walking him or buying things for him or teaching him how not to poop on the carpet.

I'm starting to think the only way to get any attention around here is to poop on the carpet. (Don't worry. I'm not going to try it!)

So this morning, I told mom we needed to have a conference.

I told her that Max and his dog are getting ALL the attention and that it is really starting to bother me and Cheeseburger too and that both of us are starting to feel like poor, unwanted animals.

And do you know what she told me?

She told me that a new puppy requires a lot of attention and that she thinks I haven't been doing my part to make the dog feel welcome and that it is really starting to bother her and Dad too and that both of them are starting to feel that if I don't change my attitude soon, I'm going to be punished.

CAN YOU BELIEVE IT?

So I told mom that I tried to have a good attitude but that I feel like everybody in this house has forgotten my cat and I even live here. I told her I just don't understand why we had to go and get a dog when we already had a perfectly good cat.

So mom said she was giving me something I could understand... a time-out. She sent me to my room to think about my behavior. She even sent Cheeseburger, who she says *"doesn't seem too keen on the dog yet."*

(If you're wondering what that means, see drawing at bottom of letter.)

Mom said that when I come out, she wants to see a brand-new attitude.

But she forgot to say, "IF I come out." She should have said that, because I am planning to stay in my room with Cheeseburger forever, which is why I am writing to you. Can you please send us a few things?

Food: chocolate doughnuts (a lifetime supply), cheese pizza, grape soda, marshmallows, make-your-own-sundae supplies (don't forget sprinkles), and cat food

Clothes: T-shirts, pajama bottoms, new slippers (the fuzzy duck kind, size 3), and a new pair of sunglasses (see if you can find the purple, sparkly ones)

Supplies: stickers, glue, paper, markers, nail polish (send lots, I am completely out), and hair thingies

When you send the package, send it to my address, in care of:

Mallory McDonald (who will be in her room for the rest of her life).

Thank you! Thank you! Thank you!

You are the best friend a girl could ever, ever, ever have!

Hugs and kisses,
mallory

P.S. THE CRUEL AND UNFAIR
TREATMENT OF CHEESEBURGER
written and illustrated by mallory mcDonald

PLAYING GAMES

QUESTION: How do you get a girl to change her attitude and come out of her room when she's 100% convinced she's never, ever, ever going to?

ANSWER: Order a pizza.

I wasn't going to change my attitude or come out of my room, but then I smelled pizza.

"What's going on?" I ask as I walk into the kitchen. Max and his dog and Joey are at the table. When I sit down holding

Cheeseburger, Max's dog starts barking. I can see Cheeseburger's back starting to arch. I pull her toward me. "I wish the dog wouldn't bark every time he sees my cat."

Joey pats him on the head. "He's a puppy. He just wants to play."

The puppy might want to play, but the cat doesn't. I don't think the dog understands that Cheeseburger isn't

having an easy time with this *second pet* thing. "So what are you guys doing?" I ask.

"Max asked me to help him name his dog," says Joey.

I help myself to a slice of pizza and look in Max's direction. "Can I help too?"

Max shoves pizza in his mouth. "Aren't you supposed to be in your room?"

"I'm out."

Max shoves in more pizza and shrugs.

"Naming a dog should be a family decision," I tell Max.

"Naming a dog is a family decision," says Dad. He and Mom walk into the kitchen and sit down at the table.

"Max invited Joey to help." Dad scratches Max's dog behind his ears. "We're all going to find a name for this dog by playing a game called the *Name Game*."

"How do you play the *Name Game?*" I ask.

Dad takes a notepad and a pencil from the desk drawer in the kitchen. "First, we're going to set a few rules. Then everyone brainstorms until we find a name we like."

"What are the rules?" Max asks.

"The first rule should be that everybody has to like the name," I say. "Remember what Dad said, *'Naming a dog is a family decision.'*"

Max frowns. "The family can *help* name the dog, but the final decision is mine."

I cross my arms. "NO FAIR!"

"IT IS FAIR!" says Max. "I want a name I like. The first rule should be that the name has to do with baseball."

"Baseball! I don't want a dog named Baseball."

Max looks at me like I have a baseball

for a brain. "His name won't be Baseball. It will have something to do with baseball."

"Why would you want to name a dog after something that has to do with baseball?" I ask Max.

Max shrugs. "Why would you name a cat after a food?"

"Cheeseburger is named after my favorite food." I hug Cheeseburger.

"It's a dumb name for a cat."

"IS NOT!"

"IS TOO!"

"THAT'S ENOUGH!" Dad puts his fingers in his mouth and whistles.

"Rule number one of the *Name Game*: the name has to relate to baseball. Rule number two: no fighting." Dad looks at Max and me. "Let's work together."

"Fine." Max says *fine* like working with me is only fine because Dad said he has to.

I came out of my room with a new attitude. But I think Max needs to go to his room to fix his. I'm trying to help, and he's not acting like he cares if I do.

Dad pushes the pad and pen into the middle of the table. "OK, the last thing we need is a secretary, and then we're ready to play. Any volunteers?"

I grab the pad. "I'll be the secretary." I give Mom and Dad an *I'm-trying-to-get-along-with-Max* look. But I don't think Mom and Dad understand that getting along with Max isn't easy.

Dad snaps his fingers. "How about Babe? Like Babe Ruth, the baseball player."

If you ask me, it sounds like a baby, but I write Babe on the sheet of paper.

"What about Shortstop?" says Mom.

I've never heard of a dog named Shortstop. Still, as the official secretary,

I add Shortstop to the list.

"How about Home Run?" says Joey. "I think that's a great name for a dog."

I write Home Run on the paper in front of me, but it sounds silly to me.

"They're all good names," says Max. "But none of them seem just right."

I rub my forehead to help me think. "How about Hot Dog?" I write the word Hot Dog in big letters across the top of the list. "I think that name is just right."

"How is the name Hot Dog just right?" asks Max.

I explain. "Both pets will be named after foods. Since Cheeseburger and Hot Dog are sort of like brother and sister, it makes sense."

Max scratches his head. I can't tell if he's thinking or if he has fleas. "What does Hot Dog have to do with baseball?"

I feel like I'm talking to an alien from outer space who has never been to a baseball game. "You eat hot dogs at the ballpark."

Max reaches across the table and crosses Hot Dog off the list. "I don't like it. It's weird to have two pets named after food."

"Max should at least consider my suggestion," I say to Mom and Dad.

Mom nods. "Max, consider all the names."

I add Hot Dog to the list again, but Max puts his head on the table. "Finding a name is really hard," he says.

"You'll know the right name when you hear it," says Joey. He looks like he feels sorry for Max, but I don't. I'm trying to help Max, and he considered everybody's names but mine. Mom said this would be a family dog, but I think Max forgot that.

Max picks his head up. "I've got

it . . . Champ! Farmer Frank said this dog is a real champ. It's a perfect name because he's a *champ,* and it has to do with baseball."

"I like it," says Dad.

"So do I," says Mom.

"Me too," says Joey.

Max holds his dog in the air. "Champ, how do you like your name?"

Champ barks.

Dad pats him on the head. "I think he loves it."

Maybe Champ loves his new name, but I don't. "Shouldn't we all get to help pick?" I ask.

Mom and Dad look at each other. Dad puts his arm

across my shoulders. "Sweet Potato, sometimes it takes a while to get used to a new name. Why don't you give it some time, and I'm sure you'll see that Champ is a great name."

But I don't see what's so great about it. Mom and Dad let Max pick a name that I didn't even like. Dad said we would play the *Name Game,* but I think the only game Mom and Dad played was *Favorites,* and Max won. I push my pencil and papers into the middle of the table. I don't feel like being the secretary anymore.

Mom clears the pizza box from the table. "Now that we've got the name out of the way, I think it's time to start training Champ."

Joey rubs Champ's back. "I'm pretty good at dog training. I've had a lot of practice with Murphy. Want me to help?"

Max grins. "Can we start tomorrow?"

"Sure," says Joey. "But everybody in your family should start too. When you're training a dog, it's best if everybody does the same thing."

Joey looks at Mom, Dad, and me. "When I took Murphy to dog school, the trainer told me to bring Winnie, Dad, and Grandpa. It really helped."

"Sounds great," says Dad. "Just tell us when and where, and we'll *all* be there."

I get up and dump the rest of my pizza in the trash. Like it or not, dog school, here I come.

SATURDAY
BLUES

My idea of a perfect Saturday morning is eating doughnuts on the couch with Cheeseburger and watching TV in my pajamas. That's what I do every Saturday morning...except for today.

Today, Cheeseburger and I are standing in the front yard in a line with Mom and Dad and Max. Today we're students at the Wish Pond Road Dog School.

Joey blows a whistle. "Let's work on sitting. When you want Champ to sit, look him in the eyes, point to the ground, and say, *'Champ, sit.'* Then push his hindquarters down with your finger."

Joey demonstrates *how-to-get-a-dog-to-sit* with his dog, Murphy. Then he blows his whistle again. "Mallory, you're first."

I look next door. Winnie is sitting on her front porch reading a magazine. She's lucky. She doesn't have to spend her Saturday morning at dog school.

Joey blows his whistle. I put Cheeseburger down on the ground. I look Champ firmly in the eyes. "Champ, sit."

Champ barks. But Champ doesn't sit.

"Mallory, push down his hindquarters. Try again."

I point to the ground. "Champ, sit!"

Champ wags his tail. Champ doesn't sit.

"Mallory, you have to push down his hindquarters," says Joey.

I blow a piece of hair out of my eyes. "I'm *not* pushing down hind anything. I don't think Champ is ready for sitting lessons."

I point to Cheeseburger, who is sitting nicely by herself on the front lawn. "I never taught Cheeseburger to sit. She just did. I don't know why we need to teach Champ. He'll figure it out himself."

"I bet I can get him to sit," says Max.

I roll my eyes. "Want to bet?"

Max flicks a piece of fuzz off his sweatshirt. "Sure. I'll bet you all my afternoon chores I can get Champ to sit on the first try."

"And what happens if he doesn't?" I ask.

"If Champ sits the first time I tell him to, you have to do all my chores. If he doesn't, I'll do yours."

77

I think about my unmade bed and the stack of dishes in the sink. "It's a bet!"

Mom shakes her head. "This is silly."

"We're working together to train Champ," says Dad. "There's no need to bet."

"I don't care if we bet," says Max. "It's up to Mallory."

I like the idea of Max doing my chores. I shake his hand. "It's Mallory vs. Max in the *Who-Can-Get-Champ-to-Sit-First* Contest."

"OK." Joey blows his whistle. "May the best man or woman win."

I cross my toes. I hope the winner of this bet is a woman.

Max looks Champ in the eye. "Champ, sit." He talks in a low, steady voice. He points to the ground. Then he pushes his hindquarters down with his finger.

Champ stops wagging his tail. He looks

down at the ground.

No Champ, don't do it! I try to send the message from my brain to his. But I don't think Champ and I have ESP. Champ sits. Right next to Cheeseburger!

"Yes!" Max jumps in the air and makes a victory sign with his arms. "I win! I win the bet." He pets Champ on the back. "Good boy," he says to Champ.

Max high-fives Joey. "Yes! I knew he could do it. Way to go, Champ!"

I look down at Champ sitting next to Cheeseburger. Usually, Cheeseburger gets nervous when Champ gets close to her. But today she doesn't. She's just sitting there like she's not sure how she feels about Champ.

Champ barks softly, but Cheeseburger doesn't move.

"The only reason Champ sat is because

he wanted to be next to Cheeseburger. He wants to play with her!" I say.

"Sitting is sitting," says Max. He pats me on the back. "Don't forget to take out the trash after you sweep the garage." Max laughs like a windup toy that won't stop.

"Max, that's enough." Dad gives him a stern look.

Max clears his throat. "Sorry. I'm just

really happy that Champ learned to sit."

Joey rubs Champ behind the ears. "It took Murphy a whole week of dog school to learn to sit. Champ sure is a smart dog."

"Can we teach him some more tricks?" Max asks Joey.

"Sure! We can teach him to lie down and roll over."

Mom puts her arm around Max. "Soon you'll have a well-trained dog." She smiles at Joey. "You run an excellent dog school."

"School!" Max looks at Mom. "Do you think I can bring Champ to school?"

Mom nods her head. "I don't see why not. I'm sure everyone at Fern Falls Elementary will love meeting Champ."

"Awesome!" Max looks like he just hit a home run.

Max might think taking Champ to school is a grand-slam idea, but I don't. "Mom, I never took Cheeseburger to school. I don't know why Max gets to take Champ."

"Mallory, you never asked if you could take Cheeseburger to school," Mom says.

"This will be great," Max says to Joey. "We can teach Champ some more tricks so he'll be ready to go to school really soon."

Joey nods like he thinks that's a great idea. But I don't. More tricks mean more dog school. I put my hands on my hips. "Haven't we had enough dog school for one day?" I ask.

"You probably have," says Max. "You have chores to do."

"Dad!" I give him my *sweeping-the-garage-is-no-way-to-spend-my-Saturday* look. Dad puts his arm around me. "Sweet Potato, a deal is a deal. You shook on it."

I scoop up Cheeseburger and march off toward the garage.

"Maybe we can teach Champ to shake hands. Everyone at school will love that," I hear Joey say to Max.

"*Awesome!*" Max says to Joey.

I open the door to the garage and look inside. Everything looks dark and dusty. I hear Max and Joey laughing in the front yard. If you ask me, this isn't *awesome*. This is *terrible!*

I put Cheeseburger on top of a pile of boxes. She stretches and lies down like she likes it in here as much as she likes being on my bed. Maybe she likes it in here, but I don't.

I find a broom and start sweeping. Then, I start thinking.

Before Champ came along, I used to

play with Joey on Saturday afternoons. But now, he's busy with Max. I finish sweeping, then I pick up Cheeseburger. "We're going to find someone else to play with," I say out loud.

I march into the kitchen and dial my desk mate Pamela's phone number. I wait for the phone to ring. Pamela answers.

"Hi, Pamela. It's Mallory." I use my *cheery phone* voice.

"Hi, Mallory. What are you doing?"

"I'm not doing anything, and I wanted to see if you could come over and play." I talk in my *super cheery phone* voice. I really want Pamela to come over.

"That sounds like fun," says Pamela, "but I can't. I have violin lessons."

"Oh." I guess I don't say *oh* in a cheery voice because Pamela asks me if something is the matter.

I tell her about my Saturday. I tell her about dog school and about sweeping the garage. I tell her it hasn't been such a great day for me.

"Hmmm," says Pamela. "Sounds to me like you've got Saturday Blues."

"Saturday Blues?"

"I'll explain when I see you at school on Monday. Time for violin lessons."

"See ya." I try to say good-bye in a cheery voice. But when I hang up, I don't feel so cheery.

I look out the window at Joey and Max playing with their dogs. They're outside having fun, and I'm stuck inside with something that sounds like a disease.

I think about Saturday Blues. I don't need Pamela to explain what they are. I know I've got them.

A NEW TUNE

"Letter for Mallory McDonald." Mom hands out mail like she's a postman.

It's from Mary Ann. I grab the envelope from Mom and head to my room.

"Let's go," says Max.

"Where are we going?" I ask. I just got home from school, and the only place I want to go is to my room to read my letter.

"We're going to see Dr. Alvarez." Mom picks up her purse. "Champ is getting a checkup before Max takes him to school tomorrow."

For the past three weeks, *all* Max and Joey have been doing is training Champ so Max can take him to school.

They taught Champ to sit.

They taught Champ to roll over.

They even taught Champ to shake hands.

When I asked Max if I could help train Champ too, he told me that he and Joey are *The Dog Training Duo.*

He said they did NOT want to be *The Dog Training Trio.*

If you ask me, Max is acting like he forgot he has a sister, and Joey is acting like he forgot he's my friend. At least I have Mary Ann.

I slide into the backseat of Mom's van next to Max and Champ and open my letter from my best friend.

Dear Mallory,

Hi! Hi! Hi! I got your letter and showed Mom the list of all the stuff you asked me to get you. (I hope you don't mind that I showed her your letter, but I needed her to take me shopping because it was a lot of stuff to carry myself.)

When Mom read your letter, she said we weren't going shopping. She said I couldn't send you the stuff you asked for. (Sometimes moms can be REALLY mean!)

I told her that it was an E-MER-GEN-CY and that you and Cheeseburger would probably starve to death if I didn't send stuff soon, soon, soon.

But Mom said she was sure you wouldn't stay in your room forever. (Was she right? Are you still there?)

And then she said you should change your tune. Do you know what that means?

(I had no idea, so I asked Mom to explain.) She said it means you should get a new attitude, and she means about the dog.

She says you're lucky to have a cute, little puppy and that you should smile and have fun with it. She says that's what kids are supposed to do when they get a puppy.

OK. I have to go to hip-hop. Write back and tell me if you have a new tune yet.

Tra-la-la-la-la!

Love, Mary Ann

I crumple up Mary Ann's letter and shove it into my pocket. Nobody, not even my best friend, understands how hard it is to live with Max and Champ.

Mom pulls into the parking lot of Dr. Alvarez's office, and we take Champ inside. The receptionist tells us to have a seat in the waiting room.

"What do you think of my new puppy?" Max says to her.

"He's adorable." She smiles at Max.

Max smiles back and pats Champ on the head, but I frown.

Max is the one who needs a new tune. Not me! The only song he ever sings is *"Everyone Pay Attention to Me and My Dog,"* and I'm getting sick of that song.

"Champ McDonald." A nurse in a white hat and uniform calls out Champ's name, and leads us down the hall. We go into examining room number three. She tells Max to hold Champ on the examining table. "The veterinarian will be right with you."

"The veterinarian is here." Dr. Alvarez walks into the room and grins. "How's Champ today?" Dr. Alvarez looks happy to see Champ, but Champ doesn't look happy to see Dr. Alvarez. He tries to hide inside Max's sweatshirt.

Dr. Alvarez rubs Champ's back.

"Dr. Alvarez, I have a dog joke," I say. "What should a person do if they have a sick dog?"

"What's that, Mallory?" Dr. Alvarez rubs the fur behind Champ's ears.

"Take him to the dogtor!"

Dr. Alvarez smiles. "I love good dog jokes. But taking a puppy to the doctor is no laughing matter. Sometimes they get scared. They're like little babies."

I never thought of Champ as a little baby before. I look at him next to Dr. Alvarez. His nose is quivering, and his legs are shaking. I remember when I was little, I used to be scared to go to the doctor. Sometimes, I still am.

"So what can I do for you today?" Dr. Alvarez asks Mom.

"I'm taking Champ to school tomorrow," says Max. "Mom said she wants to make sure everything is OK."

"Good idea." Dr. Alvarez looks in Champ's ears. He does all the same stuff to Champ that my doctor does to me when I go for a checkup. He listens to his heart and lungs, checks inside his mouth, and squeezes his tummy.

He looks at Max. "There are some rules I want you to follow when you take Champ to school tomorrow. If you do, I think Champ will get an A+ on his first day of school.

"Rule #1: Hold on to Champ. He might get nervous around all those kids.

"Rule #2: Don't give him anything to eat or drink when you get to school." Dr.

Alvarez smiles. "You wouldn't want him to leave any surprises in the classroom.

"Rule #3: Walk him before you take him into your classroom. I call that the *just-in-case* rule." Dr. Alvarez pats Max on the back. "Can you handle it?"

Max nods. "No problem."

"You have to remember that puppies are a lot like people," says Dr. Alvarez.

"Sometimes they're scared to try new things."

Sometimes I'm scared to try new things too. I remember how scared I felt on my first day of school. I've never thought about Champ as a person before. I think about what Mary Ann said in her letter, about changing my tune. Maybe I do need a new tune when it comes to Champ.

We say good-bye to Dr. Alvarez, and
Max carries Champ out to the car.

"Tomorrow is a big day for Champ," Max
says as Mom drives out of the parking lot.

It's a big day for Max too. Everybody in
Max's class is going to meet Champ. I think
about my new tune. Maybe now is a good
time to start singing it. "Max, do you think
I could take Champ to my classroom too?"

Max looks like I asked him to jump off
the Empire State Building. "NO WAY!"

"Please?" I ask in my *new-tune* voice. "I
would love for my class to meet Champ."

I reach over and rub Champ's back. Max
pulls Champ to his side of the back seat.

Mom looks in the rearview mirror. "Max,
I think it would be nice for Mallory to take
Champ to her classroom." She gives Max
an *I'm-hoping-you'll-change-your-mind-
without-my-having-to-ask-again* look.

Max looks like he just struck out. "Fine. Mallory can take Champ to her class, but she has to follow all of Dr. Alvarez's rules."

"No problem." I can't believe Max said yes. Maybe I'm not the only one changing my tune. I can't wait to call Pamela and tell her. "I promise I'll follow all of Dr. Alvarez's rules," I say, but Max doesn't look convinced.

I raise my right hand like I've seen people do in courtrooms on TV. "I, Mallory McDonald, do solemnly swear to follow every single one of Dr. Alvarez's rules."

Max takes a deep breath. "I'll be the judge of that," he tells me.

SHOW AND SMELL

Rub-a-dub-dub, there's a dog in my tub!

Actually, it's Max's bathtub too. I never pictured a dog in there. "What are you doing?" I ask Max.

He pours water over Champ's head. "I want Champ to smell good when he goes to school today."

I start to tell Max that dogs don't belong in the tub, but then I remember my new tune. "Want to use some of my Mango Madness Shampoo? It smells yummy."

"You don't think it'll be weird if Champ smells like a mango?" says Max.

"Nope." I squirt Mango Madness on Champ's back and rub it around. Champ is covered in white bubbles.

"He looks more like a sheep than a dog," says Max.

"You can tell everybody at school he's a sheepdog." I laugh at my joke.

Max looks serious. "Dad is bringing Champ to me after lunch. I'm showing him to my class. Then I'm bringing him to you to show to your class."

Max rinses Champ off, then takes him out of the tub. He starts drying him off with a towel. "You have to follow Dr. Alvarez's rules: hold on to him, don't give him anything to eat or drink, and walk him before you take him into your classroom."

I nod. "Nothing will go wrong."

Max fastens Champ's collar around his neck. "Nothing will go wrong if you follow the rules."

Mom comes into the bathroom and takes a picture of Max holding Champ. "So you'll always remember Champ's first day of school," she says to Max.

After breakfast, Max and I walk to school with Joey. "So today's the big day," Joey says to Max. "Did Champ get a good night's sleep?"

Max nods. "I hope Champ does a good job when he does his tricks."

"I'm sure he will," says Joey.

I clear my throat. "Did Max tell you I get to take Champ to our class?"

Joey looks at Max like that's something big that Max forgot to tell him. "Do you know how to make him sit and shake paws and roll over?" Joey asks me.

I shake my head. "I'm not going to do any tricks with him."

"I can help you do some tricks if you want me to," says Joey.

"No thanks." I don't want Joey to be the one who shows Champ to my class. I want to be the one who does the showing.

We walk in the front gate of Fern Falls Elementary. "See you after lunch," Max says. Joey and I walk into our classroom.

"Good morning, class," says Mrs. Daily. "Let's all take our seats and get started."

My desk mate Pamela leans over to my side of the desk. "Where's Champ?"

I start to tell Pamela he's coming after lunch, but Mrs. Daily stops me. "Mallory, why don't you tell the class about the

visitor you're bringing this afternoon for Show and Tell." Everyone turns around to look at me.

"I'm bringing Champ." I pause. I'm not sure how to say who Champ is to me. I don't feel like he's my dog, and I don't want to say he's my brother's dog.

"Champ is a dog," I tell the class.

Lots of kids start talking about their dogs. Pete tells the class that his dog just had puppies. Adam says he can imitate his dog and starts barking.

Mrs. Daily taps her desk frog, Chester, which is what she does when she wants the class to get quiet. He croaks, and the class stops talking. "Let's work on math and spelling," says Mrs. Daily. "After lunch, you'll have a chance to share some stories about your furry friends."

"I can't wait to meet Champ," Pamela

whispers to me.

I can't wait to introduce Champ!

At lunch, the kids in my class want to know all about Champ. "Does he sleep in your room?" Grace asks me.

"He sleeps in the laundry room." Joey answers Grace's question before I get a chance to. He says *"in the laundry room"* like Champ sleeps in *his* laundry room.

"How often do you feed him?" Zack wants to know.

"Twice a day." Joey answers the question before I can even open my mouth. He says *"twice a day"* like he's the one who feeds Champ twice a day.

"Is it hard to train a puppy? I bet it is," says April.

"Not at all," says Joey. "Champ is a fast learner. He's been really easy to train."

Pamela picks up her trash and walks

over to the garbage can. She has a funny look on her face when she comes back. "It seems like Joey knows a lot about Champ."

I shrug. "I guess Joey does know a lot about Champ," I tell Pamela. If you ask me, Joey is acting like he's a *know-it-all* and like I'm a *know-nothing*.

As Pamela and I walk back to our classroom after lunch, we see Max in the hall. He has Champ with him. "Dad brought Champ early. I already showed him to my class."

Max puts Champ in my arms. "Take him to your class now, but don't forget Dr. Alvarez's rules. Hold him. Don't give him anything to eat or drink. And walk him." Max repeats the list of rules like I'm a two-year-old who can't remember anything.

"Don't worry," I tell Max. "I know how to take care of Champ."

Outside my classroom, everyone crowds around for a better look.

"OOOOH! He's so cute," says Arielle. "Can I hold him?"

"Max told me the vet said no one is supposed to hold him," Joey whispers.

Max and Joey are acting like I don't know the first thing about taking care of Champ. I think they are both forgetting that I am a longtime pet owner.

"I don't know why he'd be scared if one girl holds him," I say to Joey. I hand Champ over to Arielle. I smile at Arielle. "Isn't he cute?"

Arielle hugs Champ to her. "He's adorable," she says and passes him to Danielle. Danielle passes him on to Pete, and Pete passes him on to Sammy.

Champ's nose starts quivering.

"He looks scared," Joey says to me.

I look at Champ. This is my dog, not Joey's. "He's not scared," I say to Joey. "He's excited to meet new people."

Pete looks at Champ. "He looks hungry." Pete takes a piece of leftover turkey sandwich out of his lunch and feeds it to Champ.

"Mallory, Max told me the vet said he's not supposed to eat or drink anything at school," Joey says to me.

I watch Champ chew on Pete's sandwich. I shrug my shoulders. "He looks like he likes it," I tell Joey.

Pete takes out his thermos, pours some milk into the top, and holds it up to Champ's mouth. Champ slurps it up.

Joey looks at me like I'm about to cross the street without looking both ways. But I ignore his look. He's my friend, not my mother or a veterinarian, and I don't see how a little milk to wash down a sandwich can hurt Champ.

Mrs. Daily motions everyone back into the classroom.

"You have to walk Champ before you take him inside." Joey stands in front of me with his arms crossed.

I don't remember anyone putting Joey in charge of making sure I follow the rules. I pretend like I'm at the wish pond and wish for some earplugs. I don't like listening to

Joey tell me what to do.

"My dog does not need to go for a walk right now." I step around Joey and follow Mrs. Daily inside.

"Mallory, why don't you introduce Champ," she says when everyone is seated.

I walk to the front of the classroom holding Champ. "This is Champ." I hold him up and turn him from side to side so everybody can get a good view.

"Mallory, why don't you tell us a little bit about Champ," Mrs. Daily says.

I tell the class how we went to the farm to get Champ.

"Can he do any tricks?" Grace asks.

I think about all the training Max and Joey did. "He can sit and roll over and shake paws," I say.

"Make him sit," says Zack.

Joey gives me a *do-you-want-some-help*

look. But I ignore him. Champ is my dog too, and I've seen Max and Joey do this dozens of times.

I look Champ in the eye. "Champ, sit."

Champ wags his tail.

"Hey, Mallory . . . " Joey tries to say something, but I ignore him.

"Champ, sit!" I point to the ground. Champ wags his tail even harder. He looks like he's about to sit.

Joey waves his arms at me from the back of the class. But I pretend like I can't see him. I'm in charge of Champ. Not Joey.

"CHAMP, SIT!" I say it like I mean it. I even push his hindquarters down to the ground with my finger.

Champ sniffs the floor.

"MAL-LOR-Y!" Joey says my name syllable by syllable, like he's talking to a baby. I look at him, and he gives me a

you-need-my-help look. But I don't.

I watch while Champ lowers his tail to the ground. I can't believe it! Champ is finally going to sit for me.

"See," I say to the class. "Champ is excellent at doing tricks." I give Joey an *I-finally-got-it-right* look.

But Joey is looking at me like something is very wrong. I look down at Champ.

"Look what Champ is doing!" Danielle screams.

There's a yellow puddle under Champ, and it's spreading out all over the floor. There's a little brown pile too.

"This isn't Show and Tell." Arielle holds her nose. "This is Show and Smell!"

Laughter fills the classroom.

Mrs. Daily bangs on Chester's head. "Quiet class, that's enough." She hands me a roll of paper towels. "Why don't you wipe that up," she says gently.

I take the paper towels from her. But there's more giggling as I bend down to clean up Champ's mess.

I don't look up, but I feel like Joey is giving me a *none-of-this-would-have-happened-if-you-had-just-listened-to-me-and-followed-the-rules* look.

I know how Cinderella must have felt when she didn't follow the rules and her coach turned into a pumpkin.

But she was lucky. She had a fairy godmother to make it better. All I have is a handful of paper towels.

WINNERS AND LOSERS

"THIS IS YOUR FAULT!" Max throws his backpack on the kitchen floor.

"MY FAULT?" I throw my backpack on the floor on top of his.

"YOUR FAULT!" screams Max. His face is as red as a bowl of tomato soup. "Joey said you didn't follow any of Dr. Alvarez's rules. If you had, none of this would have happened!"

Joey is a tattletale. I can't believe he told Max. I also can't believe Max thinks this is my fault. "I'm not the one who pooped and peed on the floor at school!" I point to Champ. "If you want to be mad, be mad at that dumb dog, not at me."

"How can you call him a dumb dog?" Max looks at me like I'm the one who's missing brain cells. "Do you know how embarrassed he must have been?"

"How embarrassed *he* must have been? Champ is a dog! How do you think I felt? Today was the most embarrassing day of my life. I'll never be able to go back to school."

"Good," says Max. "I hope you don't."

Dad puts his fingers between his teeth and whistles. "MAX, MALLORY, THAT'S ENOUGH!" He points to the living room. "Time for a family conference."

Max and I follow Mom and Dad into the living room and sit on the couch—Max on one end, Cheeseburger and me on the other.

Dad clears his throat. I feel like Max and I are about to get a *you-better-hear-every-word-I-have-to-say-and-change-your-behavior-immediately* talk. And I'm right.

Dad crosses his arms across his chest. "I'm tired of the fighting and arguing

that goes on around here. Ever since we decided to get a dog, all you two have done is fight."

Max raises his hand. "Can I say something?"

"Not yet." Dad shakes his head. "I want you to hear what I have to say. A family doesn't fight. A family works together, like a team. Getting a dog is about working together to train the dog and making it a part of our team."

Dad is wrong. Maybe some families work together like a team, but not ours. In this family, there are two teams, mine and Max's. And whenever there are two teams, one team wins and one team loses. Lately, I am ALWAYS on the losing side.

Max raises his hand again. "Now may I say something?"

Dad looks annoyed. "What is it, Max?"

"Ever since we got Champ, Mallory hasn't done one thing to take care of him. I'm the one who does everything. So isn't Champ my dog?"

Dad looks at me. "Mallory found Cheeseburger. She has always taken care of her, but Cheeseburger is part of this family." Dad looks at Max. "We got Champ because you wanted a dog, but Champ is a member of this family too."

Max is quiet.

But I'm not. "Max can have Champ. He doesn't even like me. If he did, he wouldn't have pooped on the floor and embarrassed me in front of my whole class."

"Mallory," says Mom. "Champ going to the bathroom on the floor doesn't have anything to do with him liking or not liking you. You were supposed to follow a few rules, and you didn't do that."

Dad crosses his arms. "Mallory, you should have taken better care of Champ. You and Max need to learn to treat each other with kindness and respect. I want you both to go to your rooms and give some serious thought to your roles in this family."

I pick up Cheeseburger. My room is the ONLY place I want to be right now.

Max stands up and calls Champ. "Champ, here boy."

But Champ doesn't come.

Max calls his name louder. "Champ!"

Champ still doesn't come.

"Has anyone seen Champ?" Max walks into the kitchen. "Champ! Here boy!"

Mom and Dad and I follow Max into the kitchen. Champ isn't there, and the kitchen door is open.

"Mallory! You left the back door open!"

Max calls Champ's name out the back door, but Champ doesn't come.

I think about what happened when we got home from school. Max yelled at me. I yelled at him. Max threw his backpack on the floor. I threw mine on top of his.

Then . . . *did* I close the door?

I put Cheeseburger down on the kitchen floor. I run to the back door and call Champ's name too. "CHAMP!"

We all go outside to look for him.

"CHAMP!" Dad calls his name.

"CHAMP!" Mom calls his name.

"MALLORY!" Max says my name like the sound of it makes him feel sick. "Champ is gone, and it's all your fault!"

DOG GONE!

"We'll find him," says Dad.

"Let's split up," says Mom. "Max, go next door and get Joey. Mallory, you go down to the wish pond. Dad and I will check inside."

We split up and start the hunt.

I run to the wish pond.

I think about what Max said. *Champ is gone, and it's all your fault.*

I feel like it is my fault. I was so mad at Champ today at school, I didn't think I'd ever be un-mad. Now all I want to do is find him.

When I get to the wish pond, I look under rocks and behind trees. I call Champ's name. I remember what Dr. Alvarez said: *Puppies are a lot like little babies.* I would have been really scared if I'd gotten lost when I was a baby.

"Champ!" I say again. "Please, please, please come out." But he doesn't.

I pick up a stone on the side of the wish pond, close my eyes, and make a wish. *I wish we'll find Champ.* I squeeze the stone in my hand and throw it in.

Even though he's only been gone for a little while, I miss him. If we ever find him, I'm going to show him that everybody in our family loves him, including me.

Then I pick up another stone. *I wish Max and I could get along and not fight.*

I know he thinks it's my fault that Champ
is missing. I want to find a way to make it
up to Max. I throw my stone in the water.

"MALLORY!"

I hear Joey call my name.

I see him running down the street
toward the wish pond. When he gets to
me, he's out of breath. "Did you find him?"

I shake my head *no.* I wish I had a
different answer.

"No one else has seen him either," says

Joey. He's breathing hard. "Let's go from house to house. Maybe one of the neighbors has seen him."

I follow Joey. I still can't believe he told Max that what happened today was my fault. I don't want to go with him, but I do want to find Champ.

Joey and I walk to the first house on our street and ring the doorbell. Mrs. Black answers. "I'm sorry," she says when we explain what's going on. "I haven't seen Champ." She looks at us like there's nothing worse than a missing puppy.

"Thanks." I try to smile at Mrs. Black, but it's hard to be happy when your brother's dog is gone and it's your fault.

Joey and I knock on more doors. The Martins'. The Fines'. The Walkers'. No one has seen Champ. I look up at the sky. It's starting to get dark. I hope we find Champ before nighttime.

Joey and I walk up to the Harts' house and ring the bell. No one answers. "I wonder if Mrs. Hart is home," says Joey.

"I don't know." When I talk, my voice sounds funny, like it's not my own.

Joey looks at me. "Mallory, are you mad about something?"

I can't even believe Joey has to ask me that. "Why did you tell Max that the accident in the classroom was my fault?"

Joey pushes the doorbell again. "I tried to tell you to follow Dr. Alvarez's rules, but you wouldn't listen."

I take a deep breath. "Today at school, you were acting like Champ was your dog. It made me mad. I wanted to prove that I know how to take care of Champ, without everybody telling me what to do. I wanted to feel like he was my dog too."

Joey looks at me. "I'm sorry if I was acting like Champ was mine."

"Ever since Max got Champ, you've practically ignored me," I tell Joey. "You used to not even like Max, and all of a sudden, you're his best friend."

"Mallory, I'm sorry you think I've been ignoring you. I wasn't trying to. I was just helping Max take care of Champ. Just because I spend time with Max doesn't mean you and I aren't friends."

"MALLORY! JOEY! " Dad calls our names and motions for us to come back.

"Maybe they found him!" I tell Joey. We run to my house. Mom, Dad, Max, Winnie, and Mr. Winston are in my front yard.

"Did you find him?" I ask. I'm out of breath from running.

"NO! And it's almost nighttime," says Max. He looks upset.

"The only thing worse than a D-O-G is a L-O-S-T D-O-G," says Winnie. She looks at me like it's my fault that Champ is missing.

I look down at the ground. I wish there was something else I could do.

"Let's think about this," says Mom. "We've checked the house, the wish pond, the backyard."

"We searched our house too," says Mr. Winston.

"He couldn't have gotten too far," says Dad.

"Did anybody check the garage?" I ask.

Max shakes his head. "I didn't check in the garage. I was looking outside."

"We didn't check the garage," says Mom. "We were in the house."

I can't believe no one checked the garage! "Maybe Champ went into the garage," I say. "Cheeseburger loves it in there."

We all run to see if Champ is in the garage. Mom flips on the light. "Champ!" Max calls his name. We wait to hear a woof-woof, but we don't.

"Champ!" Max calls his name again.

We don't hear a woof-woof, but we do hear a soft meow.

"That must be Cheeseburger," says Mom.

"Cheeseburger." I call her name, and she meows again . . . a little louder this time.

"It's coming from over there." Joey points to the corner of the garage.

I step over some boxes and look in the corner.

Cheeseburger is curled up on a pile of old blankets. "Cheeseburger is here," I tell everybody, "and so is Champ!" Champ is curled up asleep next to Cheeseburger.

"I wonder how Champ got in the garage," says Max.

"I must have left the door open the other day when I was sweeping," I say.

I pick up Champ, give him a hug, and hand him to Max.

Then I pick up Cheeseburger and hug her too. "Cheeseburger must have found Champ and kept him safe."

I've never been so happy to see a cat . . . or a dog.

TEAMMATES

"Who wants a brownie?" asks Mom. "This is a celebration!"

I help Mom pass around a plate of brownies to Max, Joey, Winnie, and Mr. Winston. Dad fills glasses of milk.

Even though I've already had a hamburger and a hot dog, I take two brownies. I don't know why, but looking for a lost dog made me hungry.

I take a bite of my brownie. Then I pour some of my milk into Cheeseburger's bowl.

"Good kitty," I rub her back. "I'm proud of you for finding Champ." I pat Champ on the head. "I'm proud of you too. You found a nice spot and went to sleep."

Max takes another brownie. "He's a smart dog."

"He is smart," I tell Max, "but he needs a little more work in the *things-we-do-inside* and *things-we-do-outside* departments."

Winnie pushes her plate away. "I heard about *Show and Smell.* That's soooooo gross!" She holds her nose.

Joey looks at Winnie like she has no clue what she's talking about. "It wasn't that big of a deal." Then he smiles at me like it *really* wasn't that big of a deal.

I smile at Joey. Even though he's been spending a lot more time with Max than with me lately, I know he's trying to make me feel better about what happened.

I rub Champ's back, and he rubs up against my leg. "Hey, I think he likes me."

"Of course he likes you," says Mom. "All you have to do is show him that you care about him." Mom winks at me. "Puppies are a lot like little babies."

I smile at Mom. "I've heard that before."

When everyone finishes their brownies, the Winstons say good-bye. "It's a school day tomorrow," says Mr. Winston.

After they leave, I start to go to my room to get ready for bed, but Dad stops me. "Mom and I would like to see you and Max in the living room."

I can't believe it . . . another family conference! I give Max a *what-did-we-do-this-time* look, but he looks as confused as I am. Max and I sit down on the couch.

"I'm proud of the two of you," says Dad. "We had a bad situation this afternoon, and our whole family worked together to solve it." Dad nods like he approves of our behavior. "I'd like to see our family working as a team more often."

Mom smiles too. "I like thinking of us as teammates," she says.

"Mom, Dad," I say. "I don't feel like much of a teammate. If I hadn't left the back door open, Champ wouldn't have gotten lost." I look down at a dirt spot on my jeans. "Max, I'm really sorry."

"I'm sorry too," mumbles Max. "I shouldn't have said it was all your fault. If I had been watching Champ, he never would have run away."

Mom and Dad smile at each other. "Fortunately," says Dad. "Champ didn't run far. He and Cheeseburger found a safe place together."

"Speaking of together," says Mom, "no

one move." She gets her camera. "I want a picture of both of you with your pets."

Max and I put Champ and Cheeseburger on our laps.

"Everybody smile and say, *'Getting along is a great idea.'*"

Max and I look at each other and roll our eyes. Sometimes Mom is such a mom. But I smile when she takes the picture and think about what she said. Getting along is a great idea. It's just not always easy to do.

I go into my room and put on my pajamas. But as I get into bed, I can't help thinking about what Dad said about working together as a team. Something about it still bothers me.

When Mom and Dad tuck me in, I tell them what's on my mind.

"Dad, you know what you said about teammates? Well, ever since we got

Champ, I feel like you and Mom have been paying a lot more attention to Max's team than to mine."

Mom and Dad look at each other. "Mallory, you and Max are both important to us," says Dad. "We try to give both of you lots of attention. Sometimes you might get a little more, and sometimes Max might get a little more."

I nod like that makes sense to me, but I guess I look confused.

"Mallory, do you remember when you found Cheeseburger?" Mom asks me.

I nod.

"Do you remember how we took her to the vet and went to the pet store to buy her food and a bed?"

"Sure," I say. "I remember all of that."

"We spent a lot of time helping you take care of Cheeseburger when we got her, just like we spent a lot of time helping Max take care of Champ when he got him."

Dad puts his arm around me. "Sweet Potato, do you understand what Mom and I are trying to say to you?"

"I've got it," I say.

"Good," Dad says. "I'm glad what we've said makes sense."

"I get what you're saying, but what I've

got is an idea—a really, really, really great idea. Mom, may I have a copy of the picture you took of Max and Champ and me and Cheeseburger tonight?"

Mom nods her head, but she looks confused, so I explain.

"I'm going to make a Champ scrapbook for Max, just like my Cheeseburger scrapbook. Do you think Max will like it?"

"I think he'll love it," says Mom.

She and Dad kiss me. "Good night," says Dad. "It's been a long day."

"I don't think I'll ever forget today," I tell my parents. "It didn't start out too well, but at least it had a happy ending."

Everyone smiles . . . even me.

FAMILY FUN DAY

I started a new club.

It's called SABGD. That's short for Sisters AND Brothers Getting Dogs. This morning we're doing our first official club activity.

I bang on Max's door. "Wake up!" I shout. "It's time."

I don't hear a sound from Max's room. I bang again, and then I open his door. "WAKE UP!" I use Mom's *get-up-now-or-you're-going-to-be-late* voice.

Max opens one eye. "Is it a school day?"

Max must be the only brother on the planet who can't tell the difference between a school day and a day when our family is going to do something fun together.

"It's Family Fun Day. Remember?" I pull the covers off of Max. "Mom, Dad, Champ,

and Cheeseburger are in the kitchen. We're waiting for you."

Max doesn't move. I wait for him to say something Max-like, like count me out. But he surprises me.

"Give me five minutes," Max says. "I'll be right there."

"Great! I'll start setting up." I skip down the hall to the kitchen. If you ask me, Family Fun Day is going to be a lot of fun.

"Good morning!" I smile at Mom and Dad and take a mixing bowl out of the cabinet.

"Nice to see you looking so cheerful," says Mom.

I start getting out the ingredients we'll need. Flour. Eggs. Salt. Powdered milk. Butter. "I hope Champ likes these," I say to Mom and Dad.

They smile at each other. "Champ's a

smart dog," says Mom. "I'm sure he'll be able to tell the difference between store-bought and homemade."

"Do you think Cheeseburger might like them too?" I ask.

Mom laughs. "I guess we could let her taste them."

Max looks confused as he walks into the kitchen. "Are we making dog biscuits or cat biscuits?"

"Dog biscuits." I pass out copies of the homemade dog biscuit recipe that Pamela helped me find on the Internet. "I think cats can eat them too." I read off the list of ingredients in the recipe. "Who knows, some people might even like them."

Max makes a face. "I'll stick with doughnuts." He picks a chocolate one out of the box on the counter.

I mix butter, water, powdered milk, salt,

and an egg in the bowl. It looks like slime.

"Want some help?" Mom takes the spoon from me and starts stirring.

I add flour. The slime is getting thick and sticky.

"Hey!" says Max. "I want to help too. It's Family Fun Day. Remember?" He sticks his hands in the mixing bowl and starts forming the sticky stuff into a ball.

I dump flour and wheat germ on the counter. "The recipe says we have to roll the dough out and cut it into little bones."

Max rolls. I cut. Dad greases a cookie sheet. Mom puts the treats in the oven. I look at my watch. "Fifty minutes and we'll have homemade dog biscuits."

Max takes another doughnut. "In fifty minutes, *Champ* will have homemade dog biscuits. I already told you I'll help make them, but I'm not eating them."

I think about the ingredients in dog biscuits. Flour. Eggs. Milk. Butter. Even though I'd rather eat doughnuts than dog biscuits, someone should taste them to make sure they're OK for Champ.

I raise my hand. "I volunteer to be the official dog biscuit taster."

Mom and Dad smile at each other. "Mallory, that's a nice offer," says Dad. "But let's leave the dog biscuit eating up to Champ."

"You guys go clean up your rooms," says Mom. "When the dog treats are ready, we can keep enjoying Family Fun Day."

"A movie and miniature golf," I say.

"Pizza and ice cream too," says Max.

"Yes to all of the above. Now scoot," says Mom.

Max and I go into our rooms. I make my bed, and then I sit down at my desk. I have

a letter to write. I take out a sheet of
paper and begin.

Dear Mary Ann,
I have three IMPORTANT THINGS to tell
you:
IMPORTANT THING #1: Champ got lost!
It was partly (not completely) my fault,
but I felt completely (not partly) awful!
We looked everywhere and couldn't find
him. But guess who finally found Champ?
Cheeseburger! Cheeseburger found
Champ and kept him safe.
I was so proud of Cheeseburger, and
not just for saving Champ. I thought she
would have a really hard time having a
new pet in our house, but she has handled
it like a true champ. (Champ...champ, get
the joke?) She loves that dog.

IMPORTANT THING #2: I love Champ!

Even though Champ is sort of max's dog, I love him too. When max first got him, I didn't think I would ever like having him in our family.  But when Champ was lost, I was really sad. You were right. Champ is sweet and cute and fun to play with.

IMPORTANT THING #3: I love max!

JUST KIDDING! THIS IS A JOKE!

But here's the truth: I don't hate max. We're actually getting along. You're probably wondering how that's possible.

I'll tell you. While Champ was missing, our whole family worked together to find him. And once we found him, Dad said how nice it was to see Max and me working together. He said he'd like to see us do it more often.

Max and I told Dad we didn't know how often we could actually do it, but we were sure we could do it for a day.

So today, we're having something called Family Fun Day. (Max said the name was totally goofy. When I asked if he had any suggestions, he said coming up with a good name is really hard to do and that we could keep it.)

So here's what we're doing on Family Fun Day: This morning, we made homemade dog biscuits. When the dog biscuits are done cooking, we're going to play putt-putt, and then we're going for pizza, to a movie, and to get ice cream.

Mom and Dad said Max and I could do anything we wanted, but that we both had to agree. Then they made us promise we'd spend the whole day getting along.

I was going to write you after putt-putt and the movie, but I was scared I'd be too tired. (Getting along with Max for a whole day will be exhausting!)

G.2.G. (Got to go!)

The scent of freshly baked dog biscuits fills the air!

Big, huge hugs and kisses!
Mallory

P.S. You'll be happy to know I'm singing a new tune! It's called "Mallory McDonald Has a New Pal." (It sounds like "Old McDonald Had a Farm.")

Here's how it goes:

Mallory McDonald has a new pal.
Woof! Woof! Woof! Woof! Woof!
At first, she didn't like him,
    but she does now.
Woof! Woof! Woof! Woof! Woof!
With a woof, woof here.
And a woof, woof there.
Here a woof. There a woof.

Everywhere a woof, woof.
Mallory McDonald has a new pal.
Woof! Woof! Woof! Woof! Woof!

A RECIPE FROM MALLORY

(In case you want to try this at home!)

HOMEMADE DOG BISCUITS

Here's what you'll need:

$\frac{1}{3}$ cup butter or margarine

$\frac{3}{4}$ cup hot water (not too hot!)

$\frac{1}{2}$ cup powdered milk

$\frac{1}{8}$ teaspoon salt (not too much!)

1 egg (beat it really good!)

3 cups whole-wheat flour

$\frac{1}{4}$ cup wheat germ (sounds gross, but dogs like it!)

Here's what you do:

Get out a big bowl. Put butter or margarine in the bowl and pour hot water over it. Stir in powdered milk, salt, and egg. Add the flour, $\frac{1}{2}$ cup at a time. Form the dough into a ball with your hands. Put a little flour and wheat germ on the counter. Put the dough on top of it and roll it out with a rolling pin (or you can use your fingers) until it is one-half inch thick. Now (this is the fun part), cut the dough into bone shapes and place on a lightly greased cookie sheet. Bake these treats at 325°F for 50 minutes. Let them cool, and they will dry out and harden. You can store them in a plastic bag in the refrigerator.

Making homemade dog biscuits is a little messy (you don't have to tell your parents that part), but dogs really, really, really like these treats. They are Champ's favorites!

Oh yeah, and don't forget to check with your vet before you give these to your dog. You know how vets are—they have lots and lots and lots of rules!

CHAMP'S SCRAPBOOK

I thought you might like a sneak peek at the scrapbook I'm making for Max.

Here's a picture of the day Max got Champ from Farmer Frank.

Here's a picture of the day Max took Champ to school.

And here's a picture of Max and Champ and Cheeseburger and me.

Mom said I should call this last picture the *Teammates* photo.

I told Mom I'm not naming any of the photos, but I am leaving lots of room for more. The thing is, I want this scrapbook to be really, really, really good. I don't want Champ to think, *"This is nice, but Mallory made a nicer one for Cheeseburger."*

You know how it is when there are two pets in one family. Someone always feels like the other guy is more important. I hope Max and Champ like their scrapbook!

Darby Creek
A division of Lerner Publishing Group, Inc.
241 First Avenue North
Minneapolis, MN 55401 USA

For reading levels and more information,
look up this title at www.lernerbooks.com.

Library of Congress Cataloging-in-Publication Data

Friedman, Laurie B.
    Mallory vs. Max / by Laurie Friedman ; illustrations by Tamara
Schmitz.
        p.   cm.
        Summary: Eight-year-old Mallory feels left out when her older
brother, Max, gets a dog that becomes the center of attention.
        ISBN 978-1-57505-795-8 (lib. bdg. : alk. paper)
        ISBN 978-1-57505-908-2 (eBook)
        [1. Dogs—Fiction. 2. Pets—Fiction. 3. Sibling rivalry—Fiction. 4. Family
life—Fiction.] 1. Title: Mallory versus Max. II. Schmitz, Tamara, ill.
III. Title.
PZ7.F89773Man 2005
[Fic]—dc22   2004002563

Manufactured in the United States of America
1-45460-39688-3/13/2018